Paper Cuts

Rebecca Rossetti

"Whatever you do in this life, know this: you have great courage, and you write beautifully. Not a bad combination".

This book is dedicated to my Uncle Anthony who taught me the power that words can have. Thank you for inspiring and encouraging me. Your words lit a magic in me which I will forever be grateful for.

Thank you.

She was the last person I saw before my eyes shut. Her eyes piercing, her smirk fierce, unafraid. Her mind was untraceable, her heart untamable, and her lips; well, her lips were my drug; and a death by overdose had always been my ultimate fantasy.

Part 1
The death

Lily

I was seven years old the first time I remember seeing the police. They showed up unannounced at our house late one night, bashing loudly on the door.

"Police here, let us in", Danny gestured for me to stay silent from across the room. I did.

Silence echoed throughout our tiny house. Mum and dad were hiding upstairs in their room; Danny used to tell me that they only ever went to their room to 'fight or fuck' but I didn't really know what he meant and the way he said it made me not want to ask.

"Police!" The knocking continued and I started to wonder why we had to stay so silent. I looked over to Danny but he was in a world of his own, his eyes were fixated on his Gameboy.

We spent lots of evenings just like this, with Danny playing on his Gameboy and me sitting across the room, watching him. I loved anticipating the change in his emotions, he was always so expressive when he played and his thumbs jumped around so quickly. Most nights, dad wasn't in.

"He lives at that bloody watering hole" Mum would rant whenever I asked where he was. I was confused. Dad lived here; I was almost certain of it. He usually stumbled into the house when I was half-asleep, his words sloshing and slurring into one another as if they were being shaken around in a can of coke. I'd hear footsteps on the stairs and then listen out for mum tiptoeing up after him.

"How fucking dare you, you fucking twat," Mums voice screeched, piercing through the stillness in the air and travelling down the stairs like a bullet.

"I guess that must be the end of the fucking then", Danny smirked, "Let the fighting commence". He glanced up at me and winked before laughing and turning his attention back to his game. Footsteps charged down the stairs and before I knew it, I was scooped up in Mum's arms, my hands clasped around the back of her neck. I nuzzled my head gently into her collarbone, inhaling her deeply.

"Get out of this house you pathetic man, I don't ever want to see you ever again. I fucking hate you and everything you've done. I was never in love with you, I hate you-"

6

"Oh, give it a rest you stupid bitch". The room fell silent. My legs dangled around Mum's waist and my eyes were in line with Dad's. I stared into them.

"Police, let us in now"! I looked over to mum and dad; they hadn't played the silence game very well. Mum slowly started to walk towards the door as I clung tightly to her body. The world seemed to relax into slow-motion then and it felt like our whole house might cave in at any given moment. I glanced over to Danny but his eyes lay fixed on the screen just as they had been ten minutes ago, and two hours before that. I desperately wanted to leap from Mum's arms and join him on the sofa, snuggling in next to him but it was as if I was superglued to her waist. She was clinging onto me for dear life.

She pulled open the door and there were two men standing outside, glaring back at us. They had matching clothes on and looked ginormous next to mum. They didn't ask to come inside. As soon as they caught glimpse of Dad, they barged their way past and darted towards him before I even had the chance to ask who they were. I watched as they grabbed his hands and held them behind his back, putting some clips around his wrists; it looked so uncomfortable but dad didn't complain once. No one checked if he was okay and I didn't understand that because my teacher had told me how we should apologise if we hurt someone, even if it is an accident.

One of the big men told Dad then that he didn't have to say anything and I wondered whether they already knew how his words slurred together at this time of night. Both of them then walked past mum and I with dad held tightly between them. He looked up at us both just as he was being led out of the door.

"You did this to me, this is all your fault," his words sounded bitter, like he was purging his body of them as he spat them out. I still couldn't tell you who he had been talking to. The door closed and mum didn't move for a few minutes or so, her chest frantically rising and falling as she tried to stop herself from crying. I was still clung tightly to her body as she walked back towards the living room. She gently placed me down next to Danny on the sofa and then I watched on as her whole body collapsed to the floor, a flood of tears escaping her eyes. Curling herself into a ball on the carpet, she started to rock back and forth,

"I'm sorry, I'm sorry. I am so, so sorry", she whispered over and over again. I still couldn't tell you who she was talking to.

It felt like an eternity before she stopped crying and pulled herself off from the floor. Danny hadn't so much as glanced up from his Gameboy throughout the entire time and I had started to wish I had one to play with too. I sat crossed legged on the sofa next to him, watching on as Mum's body throbbed with an aching I didn't understand.

"I'm sorry about tonight kids, it's all been a bit crazy. How about teeth brushing and bed?" She eventually said after she stood up and brushed herself down. We both gormlessly glanced up at her and I desperately wanted to ask her where dad and gone and when he would be coming back but instead, I dug my nails deeply into my thigh until I could the familiar sting of warm blood interlace with the air as it oozed from beneath my skin.

I remember lying in bed that night, eyes wide open and my mind whirring. I wished for Danny and I to still share a room like we used to. He felt so far away from me now and I longed for him to be closer. Danny always made everything better. From across the hallway as I lay in the darkness, I heard Mum sobbing on the phone.

"But you don't understand, I love him so much. I can't live without him. I love him, I love him…" those words played over and over in my mind that night as I wondered whether she loved Dad in the same way that she loved me. I wondered how long I had before I too would be taken away by the big men in the matching clothes. I squeezed my wrist as tightly as I could, not letting go until my hands shook. As I released my grip, I smiled as a white mark formed on my skin. I traced over where my veins used to be visible as I closed my eyes and drifted off into a deep sleep.

I woke up early the following morning; my room was crisp and cold. Clambering out of bed, I sat crossed-legged on the floor, willing Danny to come and join me there. I had always idolised Danny, even back then. He was strong and brave and everything I had wanted to be. There were times when I had felt scared of the yelling or my body would unwillingly shake when I heard a door slam, but Danny would always be there to reassure me.

"It's only because he loves us Lils". I knew he was right. Mums and dads always love their kids.

There were times when I was jealous of Dan because Dad used to yell at Danny a lot more and I would wonder if he loved Dan more than he loved me. I remember there was this one time when Dad was really about to lose his temper with me but then Danny accidentally dropped his favourite whisky glass and he ending up screaming the house down at Dan instead.

It was three whole weeks before I built up the courage to ask Mum the question.

"Is Daddy coming back today?" I hadn't dared to ask until now. Mum took a big swig from her bottle of water, wincing as she did. "Please darling. Please just eat your fucking breakfast". She smiled at me as she gently tucked my hair behind my ear. I didn't ever ask again after that. Time passed and the weeks of not knowing turned into months and the months turned into years. As I grew older, I slowly started to piece together what had happened that night. But it wasn't until four years later when a friend actually said the words out loud that it truly sunk in.

"Her dad is in prison", Bella had responded when a teacher had asked if it would be Mum or Dad picking me up that day. I didn't react when she said it. I hadn't wanted to admit that I hadn't truly known where he had gone until that very moment. But I guess a part of me had always known that Dad would never have left us unless he had to. Dad loved us more than anything in the world, I knew that. It was just that he loved us so much that it overwhelmed him sometimes; it was all-consuming, it was powerful. I longed to love someone as fiercely and strongly and rawly as he did one day.

Hayley

It's been nine years since Gav was finally arrested in our home that night. Even after nine years, I am still haunted by the visceral memory of his eyes searing into mine as he was escorted out of the front door by the police officers. I am still tormented by the jumble of emotions which fused together in those moments; the relief and grief spiraling and sinking into one another in perfect harmony.

I still miss him so much, even after all this time. He was done for all sorts of shit; grievous bodily harm on some twat outside our local, armed robbery, and of course, domestic violence. Gav was a bad man, he was. And deep down I knew that, even if I didn't want to admit it. He had battered and bruised and choked me. He had punched and kicked and threatened to kill me more than once. He had even hit Dan a few times. But, every time, without fail, he apologised.

He would hold my face gently in his hands and kiss my forehead, he would tell me he loved me and that he was sorry. He assured me that it was the stress from work, or the drink or the kids driving him crazy. He would beg for my forgiveness; he would promise me that it wouldn't happen again. And, every time, without fail, I forgave him. Before long, it didn't even feel like a choice I was making but rather a spectacle I had to perform. I had invested years and years of my life in Gav. I had invested a

11

marriage. I had invested two children. I had invested my pride. I can't even remember the number of times my friends had warned me off him in the early days. They had practically begged me to stay away from him, swearing that he was bad news. But I was young and naïve and so sure that I had seen something in him that others hadn't. I had invested my own sense of judgement. Leaving him would be to admit that I had been wrong all along.

And so, I instead allowed the cycle to continue like that for over a decade. And with every day that passed, the cost of leaving weighed heavier. And so, when that night came and Gav was taken away, the weight of choice was finally lifted and I felt like I could breathe again for the first time in years. People say that having options in life is paramount for a feeling of control. They claim that the feeling of autonomy over your own life is so vital for your happiness. But options are only in so valuable if you have the strength to choose. All that time, I didn't have it in me to *not* choose Gav. I didn't. And so, him being taken away finally gave me the space to be free. The lack of choice in that moment was the greatest blessing I've ever been given.

I do wish I would have left him earlier even if only for the kids' sake. At the time, I was so completely blinded by my own pain that I didn't even notice the impact it was having on them. Those years of yelling and resentment scarred them in a way I don't think will ever truly leave them. I've tried re-framing it in my head; I've tried telling myself I stayed there for them, to give them the proper family they deserved, the mum and dad together under one roof like I had always dreamed of having. But I am haunted in knowing that every day I stayed, another seed of trauma was planted deeply inside their minds. The flowers of who they would become were watered and grown in a forest surrounded by poison.

The night he had almost killed the young lad outside our local pub, I had been at home with the kids. I had put them up to bed just after 10pm and I was curled up on the sofa downstairs, dozing in and out of sleep as I watched Leonardo DiCaprio turn from man to monster in the Wolf of Wall Street. I heard Gav stumbling around and fumbling with his keys to get in the front door and I immediately switched off the TV and sat upright in my seat, patiently waiting for the chaos to ensue as it always did when he had been out with his mates. I checked the time. Just gone 1am. He stumbled into the room where I was sat, his eyes wide. It always unnerved me when I could see the whites of his eyes like that. The familiar feeling of fear was strangely reassuring; it settled in my stomach like it belonged there and I inhaled deeply. I stayed sitting when he entered the room, determined to appear as small as possible, wondering how small I would have to make myself to become entirely invisible altogether. I was doing everything I could not to acknowledge his knuckles drenched in blood. I could feel the corners of my eyes dart towards them and break away just as quickly but Gav was loaded and ready to go. The slightest glance was all it took.

"Oh, go on then, fucking ask me, I know you're dying to". He was slurring his words but the venom gushed out with every breath. I looked towards the floor.

He crouched down in front of me and grabbed my cheeks between his fingers, squeezing them together, tugging at my face to look his way.

"Fucking look at me". My eyes glanced up before I had the chance to dispute the decision; an animalistic instinct no woman should ever have to need.

"I want you to ask me why my hands look like this" he muttered. The warmth of his breath was nauseating. I thought about Lily and Dan soundly asleep upstairs and prayed for them to dream their way through my nightmare.

"Wha- what happened to your hand?" Within a flash, the searing pain pounded the left side of my head and I clutched my face, willing the torment to end.

"That's what". I looked back up to see his hand still clenched into a fist and I wondered whether he was gearing up for another punch. There was a twisted smile plastered across his face. I waited in anticipation for a second whack but instead watched him turn his back and head silently towards the door. Relief flooded through me.

After a few minutes, I pulled myself off the floor and tiptoed back up the stairs, quietly climbing into bed next to him. He was snoring loudly and I silently shimmied up towards him, wrapping my arms around his body and kissing him gently on the forehead.

"I love you" I whispered into his ear, before rolling back over to my side of the bed and closing my eyes.

In the morning, he kissed me softly.

"Good morning, Halys", he smiled. I searched for the glisten in his eyes which had attracted me to him so much when we first met but I couldn't seem to find it hiding there.

"I am so sorry about last night, I really am". I stayed silent. "It won't happen again I promise. I was just so wound up and I took it out on you and I'm sorry". He was staring deeply into my eyes now, his body so close to mine. "I love you so much. Do you think you can forgive me?" His voice was like honey and I was desperate to climb inside his words and stay there forever. I still didn't speak, terrified to disrupt the tranquility of the moment. I nodded and he smiled and kissed my lips gently again. As I pushed the covers off the bed and started to climb out of the warmth of the bed, he said it,

"Hayley?" I turned my head back round to his, my eyes wide with anticipation.

"If the police ask you about last night, I need you to say I was with you all evening". I nodded, wishing for him to take back his words, wishing for everything to be different, wishing to travel back in time to before we ever met.

When the police did eventually get round to questioning me a few days after he had been arrested, I told them the truth. I told them that Gav had come back in just after 1am and had blood all over his hands. I told them that he stunk of alcohol and I told them about the whites of his eyes. I didn't tell them about the punch. I remember leaving the interview room that day riddled with guilt. I couldn't believe I had betrayed him like that, after all this time. I don't know what had made me tell them the truth that day. After all, I had lied countless times in the past to protect him. But the truth had bubbled out of me that day in a way I had never thought it ever would. It had boiled over in a way Gav had never imagined it would.

Because he hadn't always been like that my Gav. There was a time when we were young and in love and he thought the world of me. He had been obsessed with me when we first met. In the beginning, we had been so deliriously in love that he had wanted to be with me all of the time. I remember him getting jealous when I said I had plans with friends. *I just love you so much and I want you all to myself,* he had joked and I remember feeling like someone had soaked me in a syrup of feeling wanted. He ended up booking a surprise trip away that weekend so I had apologised to my friends and they had all cooed at how romantic he was. As time went on, it became easier to stay in with him than go out with friends anyway. He always worried about me so much when I wasn't with him so he always needed to know where I was. He was sweet like that. He always paid for my dinners out. *You can pay me back in other ways*, he had joked and I remember feeling sexy in a way I had never felt before. We always had sex after every date, even on the ones where I'd had a few too many glasses of wine and felt exhausted but he just couldn't keep his hands off me. How lucky I was to be wanted. I knew he cared about me because he was so protective. He didn't like it when I wore skirts too short or if I spoke to another man. *You're all mine and I don't like to share*, he had joked and I remember feeling so safe with him, like he would do anything to look after me. He started to pick out my outfits before I left the house and I felt so lucky to be with someone so thoughtful.

But I guess over the years, I had driven him to become a different version of himself. I hadn't supported him enough or given him what he needed. I hadn't been good enough. I guess that was why I was so reluctant to go and visit him. I had betrayed him and the guilt of that seemed to eat me alive far more than the fear and pain ever had.

When Gav had been arrested that night in December all those years ago, I didn't know how to tell the kids. And with every day that passed, the idea of the conversation sunk deeper underground. We never really spoke about it and in all honesty, I don't think Lily really ever knew much at all of what had happened inside of that house. I know Danny shielded her from the worst of it.

Life has been better since he's been gone. Me and the kids get by. I managed to get a job in the local café and I get some benefits which help me afford the food shop. I feel so lucky to have been given a second chance. I love my kids more than anything else in this world and I would do anything to protect them.

We still live in the same small council flat on Park Road. We got given it when I first fell pregnant with Dan all those years ago. The area is fine; a sleepy corner of South-West Wales. It's a small place with a couple of old-school boozers where everyone knows everyone. There's a cricket green just down the road from us where the kids used to love going to the summer fete when they were little, begging me for fifty pence to play the coconut shy. And then there's this gorgeous huge park just ten minutes away from us which tends to be the hub of the village, particularly in the summer months. I feel lucky to live here. When Gav was arrested, my witness care officer had asked if I had wanted support with seeking new housing arrangements. She had said that it is very common for victims of domestic violence to want to move from where they were abused but not me. I never wanted to leave. Not then and not now. It is our home.

Gav was released from prison fifteen months ago now. It is terrifying to know he's out there somewhere. I was told by the police officer that he had relocated to Cardiff and a restraining order had been included in the conditions of his release. When I had questioned why the restraining order had only been against me and not against the children, the response had been that he didn't pose a threat to them. The parole officer had said that he was their father and if he wanted to make contact, then he would be within his rights to do. Gav had never been charged with anything that happened with Danny after all. I had never told the police about it and I doubt Dan himself ever did. Fifteen months have passed. Fifteen months and I still haven't asked Lily and Danny whether they have spoken to him.

Danny

I'm seventeen now. I actually turn eighteen in a couple of days. Life is good now. It got a lot better for me after dad left. I finally felt like I could breathe in the house again. I finally felt like I had the space to make mistakes and get things wrong and be messy. I guess I finally felt like I could be a kid. And knowing that he would never be able to hurt Lily in the way he hurt me was all I ever really wanted. Ever since we were young, I had this unwavering need to protect her from everything that hurt and that is never going to stop. Lily and I have always been there for each other and I know we will always have each other's backs. She is the person I care most about in the world. I would die for my sister. My god, I would kill for her.

I'm not saying life has been perfect since Dad left. Mum has had her own way of dealing with the aftermath. I guess some settle on therapy or long-distance running but Mum opted for heroin. She's fine when she's on it. It's just like she doesn't exist I guess; she just lies in her bed in a zombie state, staring at the ceiling. It's when she tries to come off it which is worse. That's when she'll snap and slam doors and blame us for the mess her life has become. That's when she'll make bold promises she can't keep. But despite all of those broken promises, I can't help but want the best for her. I can't help but feel love for the mum she could have been. Because I know she doesn't mean to hurt us and I know how much she wishes things were different. I've never seen pain painted on someone like it is on mum, so electric and so

19

dull and so loud and so quiet, all twisted and warped and scrambled. Dad spent years picking every colour to destroy her with. He carefully curated the chaotic masterpiece she became. So, whilst I don't always like the painting, it's the artist I blame.

I'm in upper sixth at school and doing all right for myself. I got two B's and a C last year in mocks. I haven't always liked school. For the first couple of years of secondary I just constantly found myself getting into trouble. I guess my teachers needed my trauma to be quiet when it needed to scream. *Let me help you,* they'd say, *but only when you're sitting still and quietly of course.* The message was clear. It's okay to be sad, but my god don't think about being angry. It's fine to cry but don't dare shout. It's important to feel, just not too much. The thing was that my trauma didn't fit into their boxes. It was joy one day and rage the next. And all I needed was to be allowed to feel it. But instead, they would keep me in during playtimes, they would shush me in the corridor. They would jot down their concerns on some spreadsheet which collected dust in a file, or perhaps mention me in a meeting once a month. And then, at the end of each day, they would clock out feeling like they helped, like they actually had made a difference. All the while I was left, slowly suffocating to death. So as the years went by, I learnt what was expected from me and I learnt how to keep a lid on the way that I was feeling. I learnt 'normal'.

Lily

Life is a lot better now than it used to be. After Dad left, it took us all a few years to find our feet again. It took us all some time to discover what life was like without the fear that the unpredictability of his mood had brought. Mum managed to get a job in the local café which was great for a while. We had finally felt like a real family. We sat at the table and ate dinner and spoke about how our days had been. I recall feeling so lucky in those moments. I remember eating as slowly as I could, desperate to elongate the time we got together; I think those blissful momentary flashes of normalcy are most likely what will flash before my eyes before I die. Those simple glitches in time which feel like peace centers itself around.

But Mum lost her job just over five years ago now and things quickly spiraled out of control for her. I didn't know if the drugs were the root of her dismissal or if they were part of the aftermath. It was another thing we hadn't spoken about, another secret brushed under the carpet. All I know was that once the drugs started, they didn't stop. And I can't imagine that they ever will.

Dad is out of prison now but I haven't heard anything from him. I accidentally saw a letter addressed to Mum saying that he was due to be released and that the information was being shared as part of the 'victim's law'. I recoiled when I read the word victim and I wondered whether Mum saw herself that way. The letter had been on the counter in the kitchen when I got home from school one day and I had secretly read it when no one else was home. By the time I had come down for dinner that evening, it was gone.

I've thought about reaching out to dad a couple of times but I didn't really know where to start. I didn't even have a contact number for him, let alone know where he lived. I sometimes wonder if Dad ever even loved me. I know he loved Mum and I know he loved Dan. He told them that lots, *I only get mad because I love you; I only shout because I care.* But he never really got that mad with me. It almost felt like he was somewhat indifferent and I longed to be important enough for him to care.

Danny and I have become closer over the years. Don't get me wrong, we fight and bicker and annoy the hell out of each other. But he's got my back and I've got his. He's the only person in the world who has been there through everything. And although we didn't ever really talk about dad and those years, nor about mum and her 'habits', we never really needed to. There was that unspoken trust between us; the silence that echoes unconditional.

My life is pretty normal I'd say. It's pretty stereotypical for round here anyway; an absent dad and a mum who is trying her best to get by. I do my best in school, most of the time that is. I want to go to uni and study psychology or something like that. I want to get a job that pays well or maybe something where I can travel which would be pretty cool. And I want to have a family. I want to have kids who never have to wonder.

It was a couple of years ago now when I first met Ayla. She was so perfectly fierce and wickedly soft. I don't believe in love at first sight but if I did then Ayla certainly would have been the reason why. Our relationship formed as organically as it can do when one person has their mind set on being with the other. I would have done anything for her, anything. She knew that. And so that was my first mistake, I guess.

She was a year older than me and very much paved her own path. She was a complete enigma. She came from a pretty well-to-do family but she was one of the only drug dealers in our small town. She was privileged although she wouldn't have wanted that getting around. Ayla's dad was a doctor and her mum worked doing something in law. Ayla rarely spoke about her parents. It was always me wanting to learn more about her and how she came to be this perfect puzzle. I had brought up the idea of me meeting her parents on several occasions over the last couple of years but she always seemed to have some excuse locked and loaded as to why it wasn't a good idea. Just over two years we had been together now and I couldn't help but feel this hunger to know her more deeply, to feel closer to who she really was. She was sort of a tom-boy in the way she talked and moved but she was also one of the most glammed up girls in the school. She gave off this aura of not giving a shit about anyone, but I knew she cared about me. Our relationship has been a whirlwind in the same way that most teenage relationships seem to be. She's the year above me at school but we had caught eyes in the corridor. That sparkle in her eye, and the corner of her mouth raising into that shy, knowing smile. It still gives me goosebumps when I think about that first glance we had.

No one knows that we are together for obvious reasons, I guess. We live in a rare time. A time in which rainbow flags can be spotted on every other street corner, where 'love is love' is posted across social media and celebrities are coined as 'brave' and 'honest' and 'real' when they come out to their fans. And yet, when all of that is stripped away. When the flags come down, when the likes stop rolling in and when the cameras are all turned off, there is an eeriness that lingers. An undeniable, 'I'm not homophobic but...'.

"I love you" I murmured softly as we both lay there in the grass, our chests rising and falling heavily. It had been just over two years of us secretly having sex in the park near my house. We came here pretty much every day after class. It didn't matter how cold or dark or wet it was. Fridays were always my favourite day because it didn't feel like we had to rush off. We finished lessons at midday and it felt like we had that little bit longer to soak it all up before going home to reality. She looked over to me and for a flicker of a second, I thought she was going to start laughing, "I love us" she smiled as she gently pressed her lips on mine. She leant in close and placed her finger on my bottom lip.

We lay there naked for what felt like hours. It had become our spot over the last year. I wondered whether we'd ever have sex in an actual bed but I knew Danny would kill me if he ever found out about us. He would never approve of Ayla. Having a gay sister was just as much a death sentence as being gay yourself and we both knew that.

"Fancy making tonight a little interesting?" She pulled a pill from her bag and a devilish smile swept across her angelic face. I had never tried any drugs before. I guess I had seen addiction play out. I know that it will kill my mum eventually. I know that one day I will come home and she will be lying in the bathroom in a pool of her own sick. I play the scenario out every day before I enter the house. I hope that imagining it will prepare me in some way, like maybe seeing my own mum lying dead on the floor won't hurt as much if I've seen it a thousand times in my head already.

I knew almost immediately I didn't want to take it. The idea of it made my gut wrench. But the idea of ruining this perfect afternoon with Ayla was just as painful,

"Umm, I'm not sure" She looked disappointed for a second or two; the kind of disappointment which told me she had been anticipating such a kind of response. And then just as quickly, her disappointment faded and she slapped on that patronising smile I had only ever seen from Danny before,

"Look you don't want to, that's cool. I'll just do it with my other friends later". She threw the pill back in her bag and started getting dressed. I had ruined our perfect afternoon after all. As we strolled hand in hand back through the trees, I couldn't help but replay her words over and over again with my every step, *my other friends.* I didn't ask her about it; my words had already ruined too much already. She hugged me goodbye about a block from my house. It was strange with Ayla; although we had been seeing each other for well over two years now and said we loved each other less than a half an hour ago, I always got the same feeling whenever it was that we said goodbye. It always felt like it would be the last time we would see each other, and it always felt like she didn't seem to mind.

Ayla

I loved the thrill that Lil's gave me. The secrecy of it all. I thrived off it. I loved the control I felt; watching her need me was like a drug all in of itself. Lily is the first girl I've ever been with, although she doesn't seem to know that. I think she just assumed that I knew what I was doing because I am older than her but truth be told, this is all just as new to me. I had never really fancied a girl before I met Lils. I had always thought other girls were fit but I guess the idea of being intimate in that way was completely alien to me. I had slept with a couple of guys before Lily but I wouldn't say I ever properly fancied them. It was just kind of the thing people started doing in year 10 so I did the same. I didn't want anyone saying I was frigid after all.

I think I'm in love with Lily. I *know* she's in love with me. We got to know each other pretty quickly after we first met and our lives just seemed to entwine more and more. There was something intriguing about her which I couldn't quite put my finger on. She was a hopeless romantic and she was so quietly optimistic about life in the most endearing way. We never really

26

spoke much about our childhood but I knew her dad was in prison and her mum was a druggie. Something like that doesn't stay secret in a sleepy village like ours for long. But Lils somehow seemed above all of that in a way; almost like she floated in a cloud of blissful ignorance, a complete unawareness for how life was not meant to be that way. As I walked down the street towards my house, I could feel her watching me from behind. I had only ever thought love like this existed in films but Lily felt it in every aspect of her life. She is addicted to love. She is addicted to me.

We live in a pretty small village where everyone pretty much knows everyone. I started dealing a couple of years ago now. It was easy money, not a life-long career. I mostly just dealt to the kids at my school. It was exciting, I guess. I loved the power it gave me. It almost felt like I was playing a character, make - believe. I knew I wasn't going to do it forever but it worked well enough for now.

As I closed the door, I could hear my mum,

"Ayla, my love? Is that you?"

"Yeah Mum, it's me. You okay?" She appeared from behind the doorway. I've only recently realised how beautiful my mum is. I guess it's a beauty you become so accustomed to that you forget to look. But she is. She stood there with perfect blond curls framing her face. She was in gym gear and had her trainers on, a pearly white smile spread across her face.

"Yes darling, I'm great. I'm just about to head off on a run. Are you in for dinner? What would you like?"

"Yeah, I'll be in for dinner but then might head out later if that's cool. Umm, I dunno, maybe sausage, chips and beans? Something easy?"

"Brilliant. I'll pick it up on my way home and then we can all eat around 7 and then I can always drop you into town if you want".

"Sounds great, thanks".

The door shut and I headed into the living room and flopped onto the sofa. Biscuit ran over to me and started licking my face. We got Biscuit when I was seven years old. I remember it vividly. Mum had just picked me up from school and I was having a hot chocolate and doing my homework on the kitchen island. I heard the door close and Dad shouting at me to 'close your eyes, I've got a surprise!' The next thing I knew, I was cradling this tiny golden Labrador in my arms. I whelped with joy. "Daddy! A puppy! Wow, she's perfect. Is she a girl? What's her name? Are we keeping her?" He smiled as he wondered which question to answer first.

"You like her then. I guess we can keep her. Yes, she's a girl and she's all ours. What would you like to call her?" My eyes lit up as I frantically searched the room for inspiration, like this puppy couldn't go another minute without knowing her name. My eyes locked on the custard creams in the jar on the shelf above the aga, "Biscuit!" I announced as if christening her in that very moment.

"Biscuit, eh? I like that. What do you think Anna honey?" I looked over to mum, desperate for her to agree.

"I think Biscuit is perfect", she held out her arms for me to hand her over and as she held her up and kissed her forehead, I felt an overwhelming sense of contentedness, "Welcome to the family, Biscuit", Mum whispered. Biscuit had been by my side ever since.

Gavin

Shoving the pizza into the oven, I slumped onto the sofa with a zoot in one hand and beer in the other. It had been a bloody long week and I needed to get out of my head for a few hours. I don't mind gardening. It pays the bills. But it fucking does my nut in hearing middle class wankers complaining that their flowers haven't blossomed this year or that their precious Lance didn't get picked for the football team. Rich people are twats, that's a fact.

I had woken up angry this morning; there were times when I felt it surge inside me before I had even opened my eyes. It was swirling, swimming, and before I knew it, I was drowning in it. It was Danny's birthday today and I tried calling a couple of times but he didn't pick up. I knew I shouldn't have got my hopes up but it's hard not when you have nothing else to think about. Danny was eighteen today. I could hardly believe that my little boy was now a man.

I was released from prison over a year ago now and he was the only person from my previous life I had tried to contact. I had spent my days inside torturing myself with the idea that he might come and visit me but he never did. Prison had been tough. For the first five years, I had the same cellmate. He was a bloke named Frankie. We got on pretty well and we had each other's backs for the most part. We got in a bad scuff once when he stole the last bottle of my hooch so I made sure he tasted blood for that. But apart from that one incident, we didn't really fight. He was doing a twenty-year stint and was only two years in when I arrived. I felt a smugness knowing I only had ten. I guess you could say we became mates but then one day the guards came in and said he was moving cells and that was that. I never saw him again. Five years of your life living in a cell together and then, just like that, he was gone. Len moved in a couple of days after that and we didn't seem to gel as well. We didn't talk about our lives and we didn't share hooch together while we played chess like I had done with Frankie. The loneliness of prison really began to set in then and it wasn't until then that I started to really miss the outside world.

I thought about Dan every day. I thought about Lily and Hayley too but not in the same way. I don't regret giving a beating to most of the people I have, but I do regret ever laying a finger on my boy. I started writing letters to him almost daily, but I never received anything back. I made countless excuses for why he hadn't responded, convincing myself that they must have got lost in the post or maybe they didn't live there anymore. But I knew Hayley would have never leave that house; there were far too many memories there.

Whilst the pizza cooked, I threw on the pads and started punching. It was part of the parole deal I signed that required me to have anger management therapy. When the bloke had suggested 'channeling my anger in a positive way', I hadn't thought that would involve me punching the shit out of a bag on a daily basis, but it did help. For the most part, I'd picture the cow who put me in prison in the first place; I know there were lots of people who played their part but the judge was by far the biggest bitch. The way she had spoken with such moral authority, the conviction in her voice when she had told the world that I didn't show remorse for what I had done. How the hell did she know how my remorse manifested anyway. Maybe I did feel bad about the attack on that lad outside the pub. Or at least, maybe I would have felt bad if he hadn't been such a prick.

They had told me he had almost died, that his life would never be the same again after that night. His parents had given an impact statement sobbing over the boy they had lost. The lad himself was still in hospital throughout the trial. He had been paralysed from the waist down and would have to spend the rest of his life in a wheelchair. His girlfriend broke down in the gallery as she recalled how she had sat by his side every day, praying that he would wake up from the coma.

I know I should feel bad about it, but the gods honest truth is that I don't. The lad got what he had coming to him. He was a prick anyway, used to smack around his girlfriend and that. But anyway, the old bat of a judge used that against me., saying I didn't show any remorse and that I was a 'dangerous man'.

I dreamt about choking her. I dreamt of her eyes rolling to the back of her head and her body going limp. I needed her to feel pain. Deep down, I didn't blame myself for any of this. I blamed her for it all. She was the reason I lost my family; she was the reason I was behind bars for all those years, and she was the reason Danny didn't pick up my calls.

Lily

"Happy Birthday Dan" I ran into his room, barely able to contain my excitement. I had always loved birthdays and I had been looking forward to Dan's for months now. Danny and I were only two years apart in age and we'd become closer as we'd grown up. He always had my back even if he wouldn't admit to it. He was my best mate come to think of it. He sat up in bed and I piled on with a crate of beers in hand.

"Gotta start as you mean to go on, eh?" He laughed,

"Sure you can handle a beer without passing out?" he jibed. We had a 'take the piss out of each other until one of us snaps' kind of relationship and to be honest I wouldn't have had it any other way. I'd never tell Dan this but what he thought of me really mattered. I guess that's why I had never told him about Ayla. I knew he wouldn't like it, and with that, I knew he wouldn't like me. I had already lost dad to prison and I had already lost mum to drugs and I couldn't risk losing Danny too.

"Let's bounce" he smiled, "I can't think of anything more depressing than spending my birthday with a mum who's more pissed than me" he laughed.

We threw on our coats and slammed the front door shut with mum peacefully lying in her stupor upstairs. We headed to the local down our street called the Red Dragon. I strode confidently into the pub. I had only ever once been asked for my ID here during the World Cup when it had been rammed. Other than that, they had never seemed phased by the huge numbers of underage kids worming their way through the doors every weekend. It was the worst kept secret that every teenager knew.

We walked through the doors and made our way to our usual big table near the back of the pub. One by one, each of Dan's mates began to show up, each one getting a round in as they did. I looked around in awe at how many people loved him. Each friend seemed like they had genuinely come because they cared about him, rather than just the opportunity to get fucked up. I marveled at the idea that one person could feel so much love. I smiled, feeling so blessed that I was one of the people who got to experience loving him. What a privilege it was.

The buzz of everyone in small huddles cracking jokes and ripping into each other was electric. There was something so magnetic about being amongst it all. I watched as groups formed and dispersed and re-emerged at different points throughout the afternoon. I was fascinated by the lulls in the conversations, the pauses which felt a little too long. I was mesmerized in watching who had the confidence to pierce it. I was hooked by the beautiful minutia of the everyday.

As the afternoon progressed, I could feel the drunkenness begin to settle into my bones as my conversation rapidly deteriorated with every drink. I looked over to Danny. His eyes were wide and his grin was even more so. This was what turning eighteen was all about, I thought. It felt exciting. I looked at him and I saw the anticipation of his life to come. I thought about all of the people he would meet, the laughs he would have. I thought about the journeys he would go on. I felt this deep buzz from within me. The world was his now and he could carve it out in any way he chose.

I tried my best not to text Ayla, I really did. I didn't want my desperation to seep out into the real world. I wanted to safely keep my obsession in my own head but I could feel it pressing on the inside of my brain, frantically trying to jump out. It was like a compulsion, needing her with every fiber of my being. After yesterday, I had felt an uncomfortable emptiness as I walked home. 'I love you' had not felt how I imagined it might. I had been saving it for months now, patiently waiting for a time that felt right, a time which felt socially acceptable. 'I love you' had been on the tip of my tongue since our very first date after all. 'I love you' had visited me in my dreams, it had been practiced in front of the mirror. 'I love you' had hovered above every hug and lingered at every goodbye. 'I love you' was supposed to feel different to this. With every drink I finished, my need for her to be close to me grew. Maybe if I just saw her, everything would fall into place. Maybe if I just saw her, there would be 'I love you too'.

By 5pm, I had caved,
'Come to the Red Dragon, it's happening'. I could feel anxiety in my fingers as I pressed send. Her response was almost instant.

'Who's there to make it worth my time?' she replied. I smiled, my shoulders relaxing down from my head.

'Me ;)'. I sent back, feeling a rush of adrenaline. I placed my phone back on the table in front of me and turned back to the group to engage back in conversation. Between every other word that was muttered, my eyes darted back towards the phone. I waited patiently for it to flash but it didn't. I picked it back up and flicked into the messages but nothing had come through. I stared at the winking face and felt daggers pierce into my stomach. Looking up to the right-hand corner of the screen, I prayed that my Wi-Fi had cut out but the rings lit all the way to the top, taunting me. It was thirty-four minutes before she replied. Thirty-four minutes of daggers wielding into my stomach, like I could feel every ounce of my self-worth being squeezed out of me.

"I'll be there at around 8." I tried not to smile but it crept out before I could stop it.

Ayla

I woke up late today and sat having breakfast with Mum and Dad whilst 'Norah Jones' was playing in the background. A slow Saturday morning was one of my favourite ways to start the weekend, the anticipation of what was to come. I rarely planned my weekends and tended to head wherever the deals brought me, usually ending up in the park with Lily at the end of the night. I couldn't imagine that today would pan out any differently. Dad called out some crossword clues from across the counter whilst Mum and I laughed as he doubted himself with every answer. *Don't be so silly Martin, how could it be wren. What were you thinking?*

I spent most of the afternoon curled up on the sofa, with crappy daytime TV quiz shows playing out in the background. The day ran away from me and before I knew it, the night was closing in. I took out my phone and started to scroll endlessly. Ping. Lily's name flashed up on my screen.

'Come to the red Dragon, it's happening'. I glanced at the time. It had just gone 5pm and I didn't want to commit to anything just yet so I thought I'd buy myself some more time. 'Who's there to make it worth my time?' I replied. Ping.

'Me ;)' I flicked the message away and carried on scrolling through Instagram. It was as if I could feel the numbness start to take over as I watched the intricacies of the lives of people I didn't know. Ping. My phone buzzed again. It was Rex, a guy in the year above me at school. 'Can I get a couple g tonight?' I opened up the message immediately,

'Yeah, I can sort. What time and where?' Ping.

'The red dragon. 7pm.' I started typing as I rose from the sofa,

'I can be there at 8. £200' Ping.

'Dope, see you there. I texted Lils then. I loved the power I felt with her. I thought about how she would smile when she knew that I was coming and I couldn't help but feel a buzz around the idea that her happiness revolved around me. I was everything to her.

I kissed Biscuit on the forehead and headed upstairs to my room. 'Alexa, play Saturday night playlist'. The beat started vibrating my entire room and I spent the next half an hour putting on makeup and scrolling through Instagram again. Before I knew it, it was seven o'clock and I could hear Dad's voice trailing up the stairs,

"Ayla! Dinner is on the table!"

"Coming!"

'Alexa, stop'. I ran down the stairs and pulled out my chair at the table.

"Hey Dad, thanks, this looks epic".

"I forgot to ask how your mock exam went yesterday?"

"Good thanks. I got an A in Maths".

"I told you you'd smash it, well done darling". I smiled. He *had* told me I would smash it. I grew up knowing I was clever. I grew up knowing that I could do anything I put my mind to. To be honest, it never really felt like I had to try all that hard to get it. Don't get me wrong, I studied when I needed to and I could keep my head down when it was revision period. But the way I heard other kids talk about exams and revision was alien to me. It was as if they found remembering a few facts to be the hardest thing in the world.

We finished our dinners chatting about our days and how the neighbour dropped round a parcel again and how we felt embarrassed by how many times that had happened. We moaned about the weather and then laughed about how we are forever moaning about the weather. It was a very normal family dinner; food, chatter, laughter. Nothing special.

"Can I give you a lift Ayla?" Mum asked as we loaded the dishwasher.

"Oh no, don't worry about that. I'll just wander down".

"Where are you headed tonight then?" Dad chimed in from across the table.

"A few friends are at the Red Dragon so I'm going to head down to join them for a couple. I won't be late".

"Okay. Well, if it's after eleven, give me a call and I'll come and pick you up. I don't want you walking back on your own at that time".

"Cheers Dad, will do", I smiled and he smiled back. "Anyway, I best be going. They'll be missing me".

"Don't do anything I wouldn't do!" Mum yelled as I shut the door behind me.

I strolled slowly down my road. The pub was only a ten minute or so walk from home. The wind was like ice. The dim streetlights had lit up the road and I could see the shimmering pavement glaring back up from the frost that had already formed. I pulled my hands up into my sleeves, wishing I had remembered to bring my gloves. I could see my breath in front of me and felt my nose beginning to go numb. Despite feeling like my toes could fall off at any given moment, I loved nights like this. They made me feel alive. The chattering teeth, the shivering bones, the tensed-up muscles. And I loved that feeling of walking through the door and feeling that cuddle of warmth hug you like your best friend, slowly bringing your body back to life.

I looked up from the pavement, without realising I had been staring at the ground as I walked. Towards me, a figure was sauntering. They had their hood up so I couldn't make out their gender but I assumed it was a man from the way he walked with such confidence in the darkness. I've never seen a girl walk like that. Not at this time. As the figure grew closer towards me, I could feel my stomach begin to lurch and my heart speed up. Something didn't sit right. He was within a couple of meters of me now and I could hear him muttering. As we drew to side by side, he nudged me. Hard. Not hard enough for me to fall but hard enough for me to let out an audible scream.

"You better fucking watch your back, bitch". I didn't wait to hear what else he had to say. Before I could think, my legs started pounding the street. My heart felt like it was about to explode out of my chest and I could hear my breathing getting louder and louder. I didn't slow down until I reached the pub, terrified that he would catch up even though I was almost certain he hadn't chased after me.

As I approached the doors, I purposefully breathed. *In through your nose two, three, four. And out through your mouth, two, three, four. That's it. And again.* I could almost hear my primary school teacher next to me repeating the mantra over and over. I had only ever had one panic attack before and I had been in Year 3. I guess I hadn't known it was even a panic attack then but hindsight tells me that's what it was. I had pushed Sadie over in the playground because she said she hadn't wanted to play with me. It wasn't hard but she had fallen over and made a big scene. Mrs Cowell had screamed at me, yelling at how unkind I was and how I wouldn't have any friends if I treated people that way. I ran away and hid behind the play shed, tears pouring from my eyes and my heart thumping faster than I had ever known it to. My breathing was getting shorter and shorter and I felt like I couldn't get enough air. I was cradling my legs to my chest and rocking back and forth frantically and with each rock, my breath became shorter and shorter. I could hear the bumble of play resume and no one seemed to notice I wasn't there. I felt like the worst person in the world in that moment, like my life would never be the same after that. And then suddenly, out of nowhere, I saw Miss Brooke's face appear around the shed.

"Ayla? What are you doing here? What's happened? Are you okay?" I tried to answer her but I couldn't catch a breath long enough to form any words,

"I- I" My chest felt like it was closing up. Miss Brooke took my hand and placed it in hers.

"Ayla, breathe with me, okay? Everything is going to be okay. I need you to breathe with me. Ready? Let's breathe in through our nose, two, three, four. And out through our mouth, two, three, four. That's it. You're doing great. And again…" When I tried to explain, she gently guided me back to breathing until I was calm again, until I could breathe and the grip on my chest began to loosen. In that moment, I felt like Miss Brooke had saved my life. Afterwards, she walked me back to class and we sat on the beanbag and she asked me what had happened. I explained what I had done at playtime and how I was sorry. Miss Brooke looked like she understood, "Ayla, we all make mistakes. It's what we do after that and how we learn from those mistakes which is important". I nodded. She went on to ask how I thought my actions might have made Sadie feel and asked what I thought I could do to make amends. She then asked Sadie over and let us talk about what happened and I apologised and Sadie said she forgave me and suddenly it didn't feel like the end of the world anymore.

Two, three, four, and out through the mouth, two, three, four. I was back on the street outside the pub. It seemed Miss Brooke had saved my life once again.

Hayley

The chill from the wind howling through the window woke me. I had no idea what time it was; I had no idea what day it was for that matter. The days had all blurred into each other for a while now. Reaching for my phone, the world started spinning and I hoped, as I always did, that it just might swallow me up. I started on the drugs around five years or so ago now and it felt like that time had just melted away since then. I really tried to hide it from the kids at first. But it had been easier to hide when it was just coke. I could still function then. I was still able to make the occasional dinner and talk to them about how their day had been. I still felt present, albeit, in a heightened state. But the very first

41

moment the smack made its way into my blood, I knew that I was in big trouble. In that blissful moment, all of the pain I have ever felt warped and moulded and transformed. It was as if the purest form of love dripped into my body and hugged my soul. I've never had a high like it since. It was, without a shadow of a doubt, the happiest moment in my life. The highs I chase now are much more preventative than anything else. They stop the weight of the crushing lows. I take skag pretty much every which way you can imagine now. On the rare occasion that I'm not high, I am thinking about getting high instead. I do not have a choice anymore. The intense need I have for it is the purest form of desperation. I texted my two dealers the same message.

'Need my fix- the usual'

I often texted both of them. It was certainly a quicker way to secure the high.

'Not until I get my money from the last two drops. I'm not fucking around with you anymore'. I had forgotten about the serious debt I was in with that one.

'15 minutes' The other replied- result. I scrambled out of bed and started searching the house for any cash I could find. The house was dirtier than it has been the last time I had risen from my stupor. I came downstairs to a bunch of cards on the floor addressed to Danny. That was the moment I realised what day it was.

"Danny? "Lily?" No reply. Fuck. Fuck. Fuck. I had promised Danny I wouldn't fuck this up. I had promised him I would be sober today. He had begged me. I felt a wave of guilt come crashing over me but it subsided before I let it settle. Four minutes until my fix. That was all I needed to focus on. That would make all the pain and guilt go away.

I started to rip open the envelopes with Danny's name on them; there had to be cash in some of them I hoped. Two minutes later, the cards lay on the floor and I had one hundred quid in my hands. There was a knock on the door.

"Here's your shit", he said, handing over my lifeline.

"But listen to me good". He grabbed hold of my cheeks between his hands and shook my face from side to side.

"Us dealers talk yeah? And word on the street is, you're not good for cash". I handed him the money and smiled but he didn't smile back,

"Look, all I'm saying is, you ever even try to fuck me over, and you're a dead bitch you hear me? I don't play with sketty thieves. No money, no hit. Simple as fuck". I nodded. I couldn't hear what he was saying anymore because all I could think about was the feeling of release I was seconds away from feeling.

I slammed the door shut, took out my lighter and watched as the flame lit up in front of my eyes. The rush of relief was instant. The world around me started to sway as I stumbled back up the stairs and clambered back into bed. My breathing slowed and my body began to shiver as I cocooned myself into the duvet. I lay on my back, staring up at the ceiling, feeling all thoughts escape from my mind. The peacefulness of nothing was addictive. I lay flat on my back as I felt my eyelids become heavier and heavier. I eventually gave in and succumbed to the sleep; a contented smile splashed across my face. This was all I ever craved. This was all I would ever need.

Lily

Ayla sauntered through the doors of the pub; she was far too beautiful to exist in somewhere like this. I watched as the eyes of the middle-aged, overweight men followed her walk across the pub from the second she walked in. That angered me every time. I wanted to scream when I saw the gawking faces of pervy men preying on her. It made me feel sick. I wondered if they were the same men telling their daughters to cover up before they leave the house because 'boys will be boys'.

She strode right up to me, grabbed my face and kissed my lips. I quickly pulled away and scanned the room for Danny or any of his mates but they all seemed to be out having a fag. I felt an urgency in her that I hadn't ever felt before. It simultaneously unsettled and excited me. She grabbed the back of my head and pulled it back towards her, seemingly unconcerned with who might see us. That was very unlike her. I could feel her tongue entwine with mine and I surrendered, feeling my knees go weak. I started to smile through the kiss. I had known everything would be better when she was here.

She led me into the girl's bathroom and locked the cubicle door; a devilish smile plastered over her face. I took half a step towards her as she leaned in and started to kiss my collar bone; her eyes still staring up at mine, our gaze locked in the promise of forever. She started to moan softly, a groan of impatience. Her lips started to make their way up my neck, her tongue circling, gently caressing my skin. Leaning into my ear, she whispered softly,

"I can't wait to taste you". I too let out a soft moan as I pushed my back up against the cubicle wall and pulled her in towards me. Adrenaline pulsated through my body as my eyes rolled to the back of my head. Her lips proceeded to make their way down my stomach and hovered around my clit, her tongue teasing me.

"I never want this to end" I whispered as her wet tongue made its way down my hip and up the inside of my thigh. It was thrilling, being there with her, in that moment. It was intoxicating in a way that only fleeting moments can be. Her tongue lingered for a couple of seconds before kissing my clit, tormenting me with the pleasure to come. I grabbed the back of her head, willing for her to give in. I orgasmed within minutes as her tongue danced around, an assured knowing of what would get me there. I pulled my t-shirt up to my mouth, biting down as the intense pleasure inundated my body. It felt like mini electric shocks flooded every nerve ending I had, my body twitching with bliss. She slowly raised her head, kissing back up my body as she stood back up onto her feet. With every kiss, my body flinched as if sparked by bolts of lightning. As her head reached mine, we both had smiles plastered across our faces. I had never seen my emotions mirror someone else's quite so perfectly. I felt like I had discovered magic in those moments. We walked back out into the bar holding hands and I felt a power surge within me as we weaved back in with the rest of the world as if nothing had happened. Was this what being wanted felt like? Was this what it meant to be loved?

We strolled over towards the bar,

"Hey" she whispered, looking deep into my eyes. I was pressed up against her and could feel her heart beating against mine.

"Hey" I replied.

"It's good to see you Lils," she smiled, "I'm lucky to have you". I couldn't get any words out. It felt like everything was finally falling into place. All of the fragments of feeling unwanted evaporated into the air and I was cocooned by a love deeper than I thought existed. I opened my mouth but the words I wanted to say were stuck to the roof of my mouth.

"Let's get a drink" was the best I could do. She smiled.

"Let's".

"Can we get a double vodka cranberry and a double gin and tonic please?" She asked the guy behind the counter. I could feel my stomach fizzing with excitement. It was the first time I had felt like we were a real couple. I never wanted this feeling to end.

He nodded and started to pour our drinks out. From out of the corner of my eye, I could see Danny and his mates pile back into the pub, taking off their jackets and settling back into their seats. I felt a dawning sense of jeopardy, like the warm affection Ayla had carved out for me was about to be replaced with a sharp coldness. She must have seen them too because I felt her hand slip from mine and the space between us grow. I took a deep breath as I felt the tears behind my eyes begin to forge before I even had time to recognise that I felt sad. The feeling of being unwanted wormed its way back under my skin and unloaded its weight like it belonged there.

"Cheers", she said as the guy handed us over our drinks. "'I'll get these ones baby", she said as she tapped her phone over the reader. "Thank you" I replied, longing for the feeling of connection to return but feeling the distance between us grow with every passing second. I nodded over to Danny as we walked over towards him, "Oh, look what the cat dragged in", Danny exclaimed as we were close enough.

"Happy birthday champ. I'll grab you a drink when I get the next one. It looks like I've got some catching up to do first", she jibed, beckoning towards the table. The rest of the evening was pretty hazy to say the least. Everyone settled into a steady drunkenness, slowly becoming more obnoxious with every drink. The music got louder and the darkness seized any last remnants of daytime. I scuttled off at around 11pm without anyone noticing. I didn't search for Ayla as I would usually do. I guess I had wanted her to feel worried, I guess I wanted her to have the chance to miss me for just a little bit. I didn't look for Danny either. I couldn't be asked with the back and forth of him trying to convince me to stay out. I texted him as I walked, 'Coukdn't find yo but I've hwaded home. If you get any drynk food, I beg you please pick me some up. Hapy birthday bro, love yoi'.

When I finally slumped into bed, I sent a text to Ayla. 'Hey babe. Couldn't fisd you at the end there. Let me kniw you get home safw. I love you xxx'. I stared at the letters on the screen

47

and marveled at my ability to hide how I was truly feeling. I took refuge in how my phone could mask the crushing insecurity I felt. It was like a kind of twisted magic; a masterful trick which played out across social media throughout the world; the ability to show up and paint and warp and mould oneself into better. I pressed send and then finally allowed myself to succumb to the heaviness of my eyelids.

Lily

The pounding of the front door woke me the next morning. God knows how long the knocking had been going on for but whoever it was wasn't patient. The hangover instantly hit me as soon as I had opened my eyes, the thumping of the inside of my head mirroring the door. Reluctantly, I pulled myself out of bed and made my way down the stairs, dodging the empty bottles and ripped envelopes as I did. I glanced around the house, noticing how dirty it was and how the mess flooded from one room into the next.

I inhaled deeply before opening the door. I felt the air enter slowly and fill my lungs, inflating them slowly like a balloon. I remember the deep sense of trepidation consume me. The lurching in my stomach began to take hold. It was as if my body knew before my mind. It was preparing me for the pain that was about to engulf my whole being. Call it what you want, but in those fateful moments as I swung open the door, I knew my life would never be the same again.

Standing in the archway were two policemen. They looked huge. The time bomb was finally exploding.

"Good morning madame, are you Lily Draker?" I nodded.

"Are we okay to come inside for a few moments?" He looked coy, almost as if he was sizing me up. I must have nodded because they stepped inside and asked me to take a seat on the sofa. One of them perched down next to me and the other crouched down by my side. The crouching one spoke,

"Your friend Ayla Stevens was killed last night by what appears to be stab wounds". I stared into the man's eyes and exhaled deeply.

"She's- she's dead?" I managed to murmur. My mind felt so detached from the rest of me in those few moments. I was a dragonfly hovering above the bodies below. He nodded,

"She's dead. I am so sorry for your loss", he replied softly. The man next to me on the sofa hadn't spoken yet but I looked towards him and his eyes were filled with sympathy. I wanted to ask more questions; I needed more information but my voice had disconnected from my brain. It felt like I was in a vacuum and the world continued to spin with me no longer in it. It was like I was frozen in time.

"Is anyone else here that can be with you Lily?" the man on the sofa asked. The words perforated the bubble around me and I was flung back into the world at lightning speed, hurtling back to my new reality. I nodded,

"Da-Dan. Danny is here". I barely recognised my voice as the words escaped my lips.

"Oh my god she's dead, she's dead" the words fell out of me in a jumble, "this can't be happening. She can't be dead. Please no, please". I heard deep, heavy sobs purge my body, my chest heaving and writhing as the news travelled through my veins. As I glanced up, I saw Danny standing in the doorway to the living room. We locked eyes from across the room and held each other's gaze as my body spasmed from this world into the next.

Danny

She looked proper mental, almost like her body was being possessed or some shit. The police man on the sofa rose from his seat and walked purposefully towards me.

"What's happened?" I whispered.

"Ayla Stevens was killed last night". The words shot straight through me and came out the other side.

"What? How?" I frantically asked, the pitch of my voice coming out higher than it usually did.

"It appears that she was stabbed in Boddington Park last night". He looked towards me and I could feel him waiting on my response. I looked towards the ground.

"I understand that she was at with you both last night at the Red Dragon?" I nodded.

"My god yeah, I can't believe it". The police officer paused a beat, letting the words merge in the air between us. I paused.

"Who, who did it?" I stammered. The silence sat there, perfectly still, for half a second too long.

"An investigation is under way. We will be asking both you and your sister to come down to the station to answer a few questions for us".

"Questions?" My voice wavered.

"Yes. You are both significant witnesses in this case so it is important that we hear from you both about what happened last night and anything that you might have noticed".

"Oh okay" I steadied.

"We will leave you both now but please come down to the station tomorrow at 11am".

"Do we have to do them? Like, do we get a choice and that?" He glanced up at me and I softened my eyes as his reached mine.

"Yes, no they are voluntary. But it would really help to aid our investigation in finding out what happened to Ayla". He waited.

"Yes no of course". I let out a deep breath.

Lily

My eyes stayed fixed on Danny as my body finally exhausted itself and the shakes morphed into trembles. He was speaking to the other officer in hushed tones and I wondered why his body wasn't malfunctioning like mine had. They both slowly made their way towards me, an uncertainty etched into every step.

"Lily, we are going to leave you now. I have explained to your brother that we would like to see you both at 11am tomorrow at the station for you to answer a few questions for us. You are both significant witnesses and hearing from you will likely aid our investigation". I nodded.

"Yes of course of course".

"Since you are under eighteen, you will need to have an appropriate adult in the room with you. Is there anyone you would like or would you like us to appoint you someone from our books?" His question felt so inhumane; the logistics of a dead girl felt so cold against the backdrop.

"Danny. I want Danny". He smiled gently,

"I'm sorry but since Danny is a significant witness himself, he cannot be involved in your interview as the appropriate adult".

"What about a parent? Might they be able to help?"

"No. I'll take one from your books". Again, he smiled softly and his eyes flitted around the room, taking in the empty bottles strewn across the floor and piecing together the things that were not said.

Danny

They finally left. The door closed and our world felt like it belonged to us again. I swiveled round to face Lily and her body was still crumpled over on the sofa. I had such a desperate urge to climb inside her mind in those moments; I was so fascinated by her agony. I tentatively walked towards her.

"Lils, are you okay?" I gently touched her right shoulder. Her eyes flicked up, venom behind them.

"What do you think?" I didn't speak.

"I can't believe this is happening". I took half a step away from her, giving space for it all to sink in.

"I'll cook dinner for us both later Lils, okay? Anything you need, you let me know". I started to walk towards the door.

"Dan?" she whimpered. I turned my head back towards her.

"The police said she was- she -she was stabbed", she stuttered.

"How, how do they know that do you think?" I paused.

"I guess by her body probably". She looked deeply into my eyes, tears brimming. Her head nodded ever so slightly. I turned back around to walk away and felt her eyes burning into the back of my head as I did.

Lily

I needed to get out of the house. It felt like I was being suffocated by the news. I grabbed my jacket from off the floor by the door and ran outside, feeling the icy cold air whip across the front of my face. As I walked along the pavement, I was swamped with memories of Ayla.

I thought back to our first ever 'date'. It was early December and the Christmas lights had just gone up along the streets. As I walked from my house that Saturday afternoon, the darkness was already closing in and the warm twinkling lights were scattered on the lampposts and through the windows of flats. I walked along the pavement listening to 'bonfire heart' by James blunt as it blared through my headphones and I could feel a glow emanate around me. A perfect sphere of magic fused together by youth and blissful naivety. It felt like I was dancing as I walked. The promise of having my heartbroken was merely a fantasy; one which looked so purely romantic in the films I had seen that I longed to feel that shade of pain someday.

We had met in the park by the swings and she pulled out a bottle of vodka from her bag. We had spent that evening sat on the cold, sodden ground in what was yet to become our spot. We took it in turns taking swigs from the bottle and talking about anything that popped into our heads. We spoke about homework. We spoke about sex. We spoke about who we wanted to be one day. The memory of her lips is etched so deeply within me, it's as if I can still feel them against mine. It was a perfect date. It had been everything I had hoped it would be. Before we left each other that evening, she leant in and kissed me softly and I felt my soul melting.

"I have a feeling you're going to break my heart one day" I whispered into her ear as our lips broke away.

"Oh, I plan on it" she smiled as she gently tucked my hair behind my ear and stared into my eyes. A car rushed past me, the speed of it pulsing me back to the present. I smiled as I realised she had been right all along. She had broken my heart after all.

54

The country lanes felt quieter than usual today. I watched my feet as they plodded along the tarmac, pondering on whether I could stomp harder enough for the earth to open up below me and swallow me in. It must feel so safe there; the silence so soft and welcoming. The world I knew yesterday and the one I was in today felt like different places altogether. How could it be that the same air that had held the secret of our love now suffocated me as I tried to breathe. I kept trudging along the winding streets, watching as the cars whizzed past the bends. It wasn't long before I ended up in our park. I guess it kind of felt like she might be there, waiting for me, telling me that it had all been a big mistake after all. I made my way along the footpath and pushed my way through the brambles, thinking about how many cuts I had earnt over the years doing just that.

As I came out the other side, my body froze. I saw the yellow tape around the boundary. My body sunk to the floor but I refused to look away. That was *our* spot. My mind was bombarded with memories of moments there; of our bodies entangled, of the sweat, the kisses, the beating hearts. Memories of the messiness of it all, of the clumsiness and uncertainty and joy. That spot had always been ours. Our love had always felt so wild and freeing but it dawned on me in those moments that it had always been tamed, carefully constructed to never leave the parameters that Ayla had created. I fell to the ground.

I must have lay on the floor there for at least half an hour. The wetness of the ground soaked into my jeans and the soil embedded into my hairline. I stared up at the trees above me and watched the wind whistle through the leaves. The cold February air brushed my skin. I knew I must be cold but I didn't feel it. I let the thoughts come and go as they pleased, I let my breath quicken and slow. I let the tears start and stop. I even let a smile have a moment. I have never felt an unleashing of pressure like it. And I did my utmost best to ignore what that relief said about me. After a while, the thoughts and the memories and the emotions began to get stuck. They came in like lightning bolts but refused to leave again and me lying on the wet mud didn't feel quite so peaceful anymore. I stood up and shook out my arms, feeling the tension return instantly.

I stared over to the yellow tape again and wondered what her last moments would have felt like. I wondered whether she was scared or in pain, or whether the world held her tightly in those last seconds, cocooning her from what should never have been. I made my way back through the brambles and along the footpath out of the park. The cars whizzed past as I dawdled along the pavement. As much as I had prayed that the world would mourn with me, it had started back up again without a second thought for the dead teenager it had left behind. I couldn't fathom how life was meant to be the same after this. I couldn't imagine how a new life was meant to look. And yet it seemed the rest of the world had continued on as if nothing had happened. It felt so unjust.

Lily

I slammed the door shut and walked towards the kitchen. I could smell bacon wafting through the house.

"Where have you been?" Danny asked as soon as I appeared in the doorway.

"I just went for a walk. I needed to clear my head".

"You've been out all bloody day Lils" His glare was accusing and I felt angry that he didn't seem to understand my grief.

"Anyway, dinner's ready". He said, plonking two bowls of pasta onto the kitchen table.

"Is mum awake?"

"Nah, she's out cold, like always. I'll leave her a plate for later". We both caught each other's gaze and I was eventually the one to break it.

"This looks delicious, thanks Dan". He smiled. The conversation between us didn't flow like it usually did. It felt stunted, trapped. I guess there isn't always that much to say when someone dies. I so desperately wanted to tell him about Ayla. I wanted to tell him about how her eyebrows danced when she was telling a story. I wanted him to know about the way her hair stuck to her face when it was cold. I wanted to confess how in love we were and how deeply I was going to miss her. But I didn't. Instead, I told him that I had a geography exam on Monday that I hadn't revised for and he laughed and said he had a Maths test too. Just before we finished off the last few mouthfuls, Dan inhaled deeply, as if weighing up his words as carefully as he could.

"Tomorrow, Lils, for the interview" he looked towards me, "Be careful about what you say yeah? These pigs will latch on to anything they hear just to pin someone for it". I nodded, unsure as to exactly what he meant.

"It's just a witness interview Dan, that's what the police said". He smiled,

"Yeah look, I know that. And there's nothing to worry about. But when they ask you about the end of the night, I think it's best if you just say we came home together after the pub." I glanced up at him and his eyes were like daggers into mine, goading me to fuck up. I didn't ask him the question but he continued to answer me anyway,

"It's not cause of anything. I just don't trust the police, okay? And if we can just vouch for each other, they'll move on and look for who actually done it". I continued to stare directly at him from across the table,

"Like an alibi?" He nodded.

"I guess". Heat rose within me and a thin layer of sweat bounced off my forehead. I couldn't help but think that alibis were only needed by guilty people.

We finished off dinner and we didn't talk about Ayla or the case for the rest of the night but the unspoken words fizzled beneath the surface of every other conversation. Afterwards, I walked the plate of cold pasta up and knocked on mum's door, knowing full well she wouldn't respond. I creaked it open and saw her sprawled out on top of her bed, arms flailed to the side. I placed the plate onto the side table and whispered,

"Here's some dinner for you mum". I could see her eyes fluttering and she made a grunt of recognition. As I turned around to walk back out, I heard her,

"I'm sorry".

"I know you are Mum". She continued, "There's things I've done. Things I need to forget". I paused at the doorway, wondering whether to press her on what she meant but I realised that I didn't want to know. I already had too many secrets of my own.

Danny

The alarm pierced my ears as I rolled across my bed to turn it off. 10am. We needed to be at the station in an hour. Hauling myself from beneath the sheets, I felt the coldness of the room zap any of the energy I had left. I plodded across to Lily's room and knocked gently on the door.

"Come in". Her bloodshot eyes pierced into mine.

"We've got to be in the station in an hour. Let's head out in 45 minutes". She nodded.

"I'll jump in the shower and meet you downstairs"

"Don't" I responded. "It's important for them to see you looking like this you know". I could hear the harshness of my words as they left my lips and I wished I could soften them somehow. The planning of it felt inhumane but I knew the police would be scrutinizing Lily's every move and I needed to protect her.

Lily

As we entered the door of the police station, I felt a wave of calm wash over me. It looked like a waiting room at the dentists. There was a water cooler in the corner with those small paper cups which only fit a mouthful of water inside. The radio was playing a fraction too quietly to actually hear what was happening, and there was a desk with glass panes with a friendly looking woman behind the counter. The lady behind the desk told Danny and I to wait in the seating area until someone came and got us.

After about twenty minutes, a small woman with a short black bob and fierce blue eyes walked towards us.

"Good morning, my name is Detective Constable Blythe. Would you both like to come this way and we'll get everything going". She smiled at me; a soft, honey-soaked smile. I nodded eagerly, a strange desire to please her oozing out from me.

"I don't wanna do it", Danny blurted out. My eyes darted towards him, panic settling into my bones. There was a silence in the air. "We was told it was voluntary and I ain't gonna do it". Detective Blythe's honey-soaked smile disappeared from her face and I felt so mad at Danny for upsetting her. She nodded at Danny.

"That is your right Daniel". She paused and then turned her attention back toward me, "Lily, would you like to come this way and we will proceed with your interview". I glanced towards Dan and saw a glisten in his eye which I couldn't recognise. I nodded and Detective Blythe led me down a corridor and into a room labelled 'Interview room 5'. There were two people already in there, sat across from each other, on either side of the table. The woman rose from her seat as soon as I walked in and held out her hand for me to shake.

"Hi Lily, I am Daisy and I'm going to be your responsible adult. I know the jargon can all sound a bit strange but just know that you can ask to stop the interview at any point and we can go through your rights if you're unsure". I nodded. "Detective Jenkins tells me that you don't want a solicitor. I can't make you do anything but can I strongly suggest that you reconsider". I shook my head. "I'm fine by myself thanks". We sat down and the man across the table clicked a button on the recorder next to him. This was it.

"This interview is being tape recorded and may be given in evidence if your case is brought to trial. We are in an interview room 2 at Haverfordwest Police station. The date is 19th February 2024 and the time by my watch is 11:32am. I am Detective Constable Jenkins. The other police officer present is Detective Constable Blythe. Please state your full name and date of birth". A bubble had formed in the back of my throat and I wasn't sure if any words were going to make it out alive.

"Lily Draker. I was born on 5th September 2008", the bubble burst. "Also present is appropriate adult Daisy Hurst. Do you agree what there are no other persons present?" I nodded.

"For the tape please", he prompted. His voice was stern, unwavering.

"Yes". He turned his head towards Daisy then and I looked over to her. She was steely-eyed, unphased by Jenkins stern voice and heavy handiness.

"Daisy. May I remind you that you are not here to act simply as an observer. Your role here is to advise Lily, facilitate communication and ensure that the interview is conducted fairly".

"I understand".

"Before the start of this interview, I must remind you that you are entitled to free and independent legal advice either in person or by telephone at any stage. Do you wish to speak to a legal advisor now or have one present during the interview?"

"No", I replied. I could feel Daisy tense up ever so slightly beside me. I knew she thought I was being stupid but I'd heard enough stories about solicitors doing botched jobs and people getting done for it. I wasn't about to become one of them.

"You do not have to say anything but it may harm your defense if you do not mention when questioned something you later rely on in court. Anything you do say may be given in evidence". My mind flew to Danny, I needed him here next to me. I needed him now more than ever. Detective Blythe spoke next. Her voice was so soothing juxtaposed with Jenkins.

"Lily, we are here today to find out exactly what happened to Ayla Stevens. When did you last see her?" I hauled my mind back to Friday night; to the moments we created pure magic in the bathroom.

"On Friday, at the Red Dragon", Jenkins scribbled something on the notepad in front of him.

"What was the nature of your relationship with Ayla, Lily?"

"What do you mean?"

"Would you say the two of you were in a romantic relationship?"
I could feel a redness escape from my cheeks, heat rising from deep within me. I nodded,

"Yeah, I guess so".

"What did this relationship involve? Were you intimate with one another?"

"Yes" I paused before adding, "but it wasn't just that. We really liked each other. I mean like, we were in love".

"So, you were in love with Ayla Stevens?" she confirmed, "yes" I replied without any hesitation. "And was she in love with you?"

"Yes," I looked up at her but she stayed silent. "I mean, I think she was". She remained silent when I looked at her and I consciously had to stop myself from filling it in. Jenkins jumped in then.

"When you saw Ayla on Friday night, did you notice anything different about her?"

I thought back to the unusual sense of urgency she had that night as we had sex in the toilets. I was transported back to the weightlessness I had felt when I orgasmed with her head in between my legs. There was something different about her that night, I was sure of it. Or was that just my mind playing tricks on me? Was it merely the nostalgia of a moment frozen in time, a moment we would never feel again.

"No". I responded, hoping that he hadn't felt the hesitation in my voice.

"Was it common for you and Ayla to argue Lily?" He continued. I hated the way he jumped from one idea to the next; like he never wanted my feet to land.

"No, not at all. I hated arguing with Ayla so we barely ever did". He again jotted something down on the piece of paper in front of her and I immediately felt a sense of unease settle.

"Did you argue at all on Saturday night?" I shook my head.

"No".

"No little tiffs or anything that upset you at all?" My stomach twisted as my mind flashed back; the tears streaming down my face as I stormed away.

"No".

"What time did you leave the pub on Saturday night?"

"Umm I dunno, about eleven, I guess"

"And did Ayla leave with you?" I shook my head,

"No, I couldn't find her". I could feel my voice beginning to waver. I needed it to steady inside my throat.

"How did you get home?"

"I walked. It's not far".

"I see, and were you alone? Or did you leave with someone?" I could feel the sweat begin to form crystals on the back of my neck. I tried to open my mouth but then closed it again.

"Lily?" he prompted.

"I left with Danny, my brother". He looked up at me, his eyes meeting mine. I could feel the magnitude of what I had just said settle like dust in the room. There was no going back now. I wondered if he could smell the fear exuding from the drops of my sweat. Again, he jotted something down on the piece of paper in front of him. His face was a blank canvas, expressionless.

"So, you're saying that Daniel left at the same time as you then, is that correct?"

"Yeah" The sweat must be obvious by now, it felt like my whole head was on fire. Blythe took over then and the interview went on for another thirty minutes or so but the questions felt easier to handle from that moment on. She asked me about how we met and there were moments when I forgot I was in an interview altogether. It felt like sharing my favourite love story with strangers at a bar. For those fleeting moments, it felt like I was finally able to celebrate us and everything we had been. I felt such a power in controlling the narrative of what we had. She asked me about the drugs and if I had played a role in her dealing. And then she asked me if Ayla has any enemies, if there was anyone who might want to hurt her.

"Does Ayla have any enemies that you know of? Anyone who might want to hurt her?" Again, my mind whirred. I was sure Ayla had plenty of enemies. There was bound to be several people who had experienced moments of conflict in their grief. There must be many people who had prayed for her to die and felt a twisted sort of responsibility now that she was dead. Because while we so often worship the deceased like they had never done wrong, we tend to forget the complexities of relationships we had when they were living. I shook my head.

"No, no one. Everyone loved Ayla".

"Lily, is there anything else you can think of that might be useful for us to know?" I shook my head,

"No, I can't think of anything".

"Okay. Under the Police and Criminal Evidence Act of 1984, we will be seizing your phone as we believe it could contain vital information that is relevant to this investigation". My brain felt like it was about to explode.

"What, why?" I could hear the exasperation escape with the words and I prayed that they couldn't hear it too.

"Since you and Ayla were in a relationship, there could be useful information that gives us some insight into what may have happened on Friday night".

"But why can't you just look at Ayla's phone?" There was a pause. "Ayla's phone has not been located. It wasn't on her body when we found her". Everything slowed. Ayla always had her phone with her. Her phone had to be with her, it had to be. I was frozen.

"Lily?" I was pulled back into the room, "we will need to seize your phone. We will let you know when it is ready to collect". I nodded.

"The time is 12:21pm and the interview with witness Lily Draker is concluded". I heard Daisy let out an audible sigh from next to me and I wondered what could possibly have warranted any feelings of stress for her.

As I walked out of the interview room, I felt a wave of relief wash over me. I would get to see Danny now. I would be able to tell him that I had done good, that I had said we left the pub together just like he had told me to. I would be able to tell him that they believed it. A cloak of pride covered me. But as I walked around the corner into the waiting area, Danny was nowhere to be seen.

Hayley

I heard the door slam and glanced over to the clock. 11:42am. The heaviness of his feet stomping up the stairs told me that it must be Danny. Where the hell had he been so early on a Sunday? Forcing myself up, I heaved my decaying body over to his bedroom door. "Danny darling, are you okay? Where have you been?" Silence. "Danny?" I could almost feel the distain he had for me seeping underneath the crack in the door. Silence. I slowly began to push it open,

"Oh, fucking get lost will you mum". I paused; the door halfway open. I wish he knew how lost I truly felt, how far detached I was from the person I once was. We live in an age where people are constantly trying to 'find themselves' and yet all I have *ever* craved is to lose myself completely. I would rather be anywhere else in the world but inside my own head. It is the place I feel the least safe, constantly swarmed by the cruelest of thoughts. I pushed on, opening the door and taking a few steps towards him. He was lying face down on his bed, scrolling through Instagram. I could see flashes of new clothes, of barely dressed girls, of money. He can't have looked at one photo for more than a second before scrolling down to the next and yet he was frantically double tapping and the heart would appear. A heart that would too pop up on someone else's phone and give them a fleeting moment of feeling important, of feeling loved. How lucky I had been to grow up without social media, I thought.

"Danny darling, I'm so sorry I missed your birthday. I'm going to make up for it today and cook your favourite dinner and I'll pop to the shops and grab a cake and we can celebrate". The scrolling and double tapping continued and I couldn't tell if he had heard me.

"Danny?" He didn't turn around and he didn't stop the scrolling, "Yeah, whatever mum, whatever helps the guilt". I desperately wanted to tell him that that wasn't it, that it was because I wanted to do something for him, because I truly cared about him. But we both knew that he was right. Guilt was the only thing that made me do anything other than stick those needles into my arm or breathe in that smoke that taste like nectar. I writhed in guilt in every waking second when I wasn't high as a kite.

"Where's Lily? I'll see if she wants to join for dinner as well." The scrolling stopped and Danny rolled over and looked at me then, a slight twinkle in his eye.

"I can't imagine she'll want to celebrate. Her fucktard of a friend got killed last night". I felt the blood drain from my face and I wished I could have forced it back inside.

"What do you mean? Who? How?" Danny sniggered, "Oh I don't know. She was just some low-life who Lily latched onto". I could feel my voice shaking,

68

"And she's dead? What was her name?"

"Ayla Stevens", he paused. "Lily will get over it. She was just some skank who dealt drugs. Hey, maybe you knew her" he joked and flipped himself back over to carry on scrolling.

I stood for a second, my brain trying to catch up. Danny had no idea how right he was. I did know her. I knew her well. My mind frantically searched for something stable to grasp on to but it felt like everything I tried to hold crumbled through my fingers. I willed the flashes of last night to float out through the window but they came and went like a pulse refusing to die. I found myself staggering backwards towards his bedroom door, desperate to escape from the room before it closed in on me.

"I'll- I'll have dinner for you later my love. It will all be okay". I could feel my fingers restlessly reaching into my pocket before I had even made it to the door. The promise I had just made melting away like they always did. I stumbled back into my bedroom and clicked down on the lighter, nausea beginning to set in alongside a dire need to escape my reality. I could feel the fumes circle in towards the back of my throat as I lay onto my back, the softness of my mattress embracing my rotting body. The need for the high trumped anything else; any remorse or regret, any guilt or promise. I pulled the covers over me and felt my eyes rolling to the back of my head as an overwhelming sense of calm consumed me.

I never know how long exactly I am out of it for but I woke up to the sound of a motorbike revving on the street outside. The weight of the headache was strong, pounding the inside of my

69

head, as if desperately trying to escape. The nausea hadn't set in yet but I knew it would find me soon. The fear arrived seconds later as Dan's words repeated over and over again in my head. Tears exploded from my eyes. I couldn't remember the last time I had cried. I don't think I had ever let the sadness sit with me for long enough so the tears streaming down my face caught me off guard.

I wasn't sure if you could call what I was feeling as sadness anyway. It was rather a barrage of terror and shame and the unknown all wrapped up and tossed around together, fighting to claim the top spot. A moment of clarity swept across me as it dawned on me what I needed to do. I needed more information. I had to find out what the police already knew.

Lily

The door swung open and Mum was standing in the doorway. I noticed her bloodshot eyes immediately. Had she been crying? She flung open her arms and wrapped them around me, holding me tightly.

"Oh Lily, I'm so sorry to hear about your friend, come here". I could feel my muscles tensing and I wondered if that was a normal reaction to being hugged by your mother. Reluctantly, I prized my arms up from my sides and wrapped them around her back. I could feel her bones protruding from her skin and her wiry hair stuck against my face. She felt ill. And it dawned on me that I had never thought of my mum as ill, only ever selfish. She pulled back.

"Come in come in, let me make you a cup of tea". I sat at the kitchen table as I could hear the kettle boiling and Mum frantically trying to find a clean mug.

"Danny told me and I just couldn't believe it. Someone so young", she started as she sat down opposite me, handing me the grottiest cup of tea I had ever seen.

"She was your friend?" I nodded.

"Oh Lily, I'm so sorry, how awful". I nodded again, unclear as to what she was trying to gain from this conversation.

"Do you know how it happened?"

"The police say she was stabbed but they haven't really told me anything else"

I glanced up at her and I could see a frantic-ness in her eyes, as if she couldn't wait for the answer, like she needed to know. I couldn't put my finger on it but it felt strange.

"They took my fucking phone though"

"What? Why?"

"Ayla didn't have hers when they found her so they think it might be useful" I paused, "And it's weird cause Ayla literally always has her phone on her. I don't really understand it".

"Hmm, how strange". She paused, "Well let me know what I can do to help. I'm going to cook a birthday meal for Dan tonight if you're in?" I smiled and nodded,

"Sure mum, sounds nice". She smiled back and I could only imagine how that suggestion would have gone down with Dan. I pushed my chair out from the table, grabbed my mug and placed it in the sink, and then headed upstairs as quietly as I could. I wasn't ready to see Dan yet. I wasn't ready to ask him why he refused to be interviewed.

Hayley

I sat at the table for a little while longer, finishing the last dregs of my cup of tea. I took a deep breath and then clambered back up the stairs and into my room. I hurried over and pulled up my mattress and grabbed the duffel bag hiding underneath. I scrambled through the little plastic bags of coke and smack. At the bottom of the bag, I felt it. I clutched it firmly between my fist. Ayla's phone. It was switched off but it still felt dirty in my grasp; almost like it might explode at any given moment. I didn't have much time. Selling it was no longer an option and I needed to get rid as soon as possible. I shoved it deeply into my pocket and shook off the feeling of being watched. Hurtling back down the stairs, I grabbed the keys from the counter and yelled up the stairs, "I'm off to the shops! I won't be long". Silence. It was the most common response I ever got. It felt almost calming. I power walked down the country lanes until I reached the stile on the corner of the meadow. After clambering over it, my eyes flickered frantically around. It was deadly silent; not another soul in sight. With all my might, I flung the phone as far I could into the mess of hedges and bushes. Fear and adrenaline twisted within me.

Quickly, I turned back around and back over the stile and onto the cobbled lane, back towards the center of the village. As I walked, I could feel the need for my next hit begin to settle into my bones. The desperation always seemed to start there. My bones started to ache and then that aching simmered out of my bones and into my rapidly decaying muscles. There was barely anything to me now and the pain always felt bigger than I was. It engulfed my whole being. I knew it wouldn't be long now until the nausea began. I needed to get in and out the shops before that happened. I picked up the pace and darted around the shops, picking up a bag of frozen chips, some chicken nuggets and a bag of frozen peas. I sped down the 'sweet treats' aisle and picked up the most chocolatey looking birthday cake I could find. As I buzzed it through the self-checkout, the nausea rose in me as the price did. £14.31. Fuck me. Whatever happened to 'cheap and cheerful'. I didn't have time to go back and change the cake for something else so I tapped my phone and swallowed the rising sickness I could feel from within. I managed to get back onto the street before it found its way back up and I stood, my body heaving as I brought back up the cup of tea. I could feel people walking behind me and the dirty looks they were giving burned into the back of my head. The judgments from people who have never had to feel the things I've felt nor carry the memories I carry.

After I had finished throwing up, I managed the three-minute walk back home. Opening up the door, I could hear the TV playing from Lily's room and I wished for the sounds of the character's voices to drown out her thoughts. I wished for the monotony of whatever it was she was watching to immerse her with a numbness that didn't hurt her anymore. I had an overwhelming desire to kill her pain. She was just a girl. She didn't deserve to feel so broken. Not yet. It wasn't fair.

I dumped the food onto the kitchen table and then crept upstairs into my bedroom. My body was on autopilot. I prepped the needle and felt the sweet release of contentedness as the smack glided into me, an immediate cure for the illness that tortured my body. Immediately, my breathing slowed and I felt the weightlessness return again. I laid down on the bed and closed my eyes, feeling a drowsiness I couldn't ignore. The noise from Lily's TV became fainter as I drifted into a deep, blissful sleep.

Lily

I lay on my bed staring at the TV for hours. I couldn't even tell you what I was watching. All I knew was that the main character looked happy and sad and angry and hurt all in the space of one episode. My curtains were drawn but I could still feel the darkness loom in as the sun disappeared from the sky and the moon took its place. I thought back to this time yesterday. It would have been about this time that I texted Ayla, asking her to come and join me at the Red Dragon. I wondered whether the police had read those messages yet. I wondered how many of the intimate details they now knew about mine and Ayla's relationship. I wondered if they could feel what we felt through the messages on my phone. I wondered if they could feel the way my stomach jumped when I heard the ping, if they smiled the way I did when she playfully flirted with me. I wondered whether their heart rate quickened when they saw her naked body. I wondered whether they traced the outline of her. I wondered whether they could feel the power imbalance, if they could feel my desire to be valued through the letters on the screen.

I was still lying on my bed, with that same gormless look on my face staring at the TV when my stomach began to rumble. I glanced at the clock. 7:38pm. Dinner must be ready soon. I heaved myself up from the bed and fumbled down the stairs but I couldn't hear the sound of Mum scrabbling away in the kitchen. I couldn't smell the scent of chicken wafting through the hallway. All I could feel was that inevitable sink in my stomach; a deep knowing that Mum wasn't going to get better and that forgotten birthdays and missed dinners ought to no longer surprise me.

I walked through into the kitchen and turned on the oven, pouring the nuggets and chips onto a baking tray. I felt for my phone in my pocket to text Dan that dinner would be ready in about half an hour and felt that flurry of panic when I couldn't feel it, quickly followed by the sinking realization as to why. Instead, I plodded back up the stairs and paused outside Dan's room, anxious to knock. Plucking up the courage, I lightly tapped on his door,

"Dan, dinner will be ready in thirty, okay?" I could hear him shuffling around and after an elongated few moments,

"Great Lil, thanks". I smiled. Relief rushed through me as I realised that my best friend wasn't going anywhere. That would never ever change.

When the food was ready, I plated it up and shoved the peas in the freezer since I couldn't be bothered boiling them after all. I yelled up to Dan to come down. He grabbed his plate, pulled out his chair and sat down at the table opposite me.

"Mum brought a cake for pudding" I gestured over towards the counter,

"Ah sweet, I guess that makes up for everything" he laughed and winked at me. "Where is heroin Hayls then?" He added and I shook my head as he asked. I hated him calling her that. "I guess upstairs but I haven't checked. I'll bring up some food for her later." He rolled his eyes,

"She'll have to stand on her own two feet one day". I paused. The urge inside me to bring the conversation back to Ayla was stronger than I wanted it to be. I had so many unanswered questions.

"Dan?" he glanced up. "Why didn't you want to be interviewed today?" We caught eyes and for a moment, I wasn't sure if he was going to answer me at all.

"It's just safer that way. The pigs are quick to twist words you get me. I just want to forget about the whole thing now". I nodded.

"I said what you told me to", I added, desperate to please him somehow.

"Good". He stood up, picking up his plate and dropping it into the sink.

"I loved her you know. Like, I was in love with her". I could feel his body freeze, the back of his head tense up. He turned back around.

"I know you did. But she's dead now so we all need to just move on and get on with life". His words cut through me. I was so desperately trying to believe she could still be alive somehow, in some shape. His words stole that possibility. Dead. She would now only ever be remembered as the girl who was murdered. And I guess I would now only ever be the girlfriend of the girl who was murdered.

Gavin

I waited in the corridor for the therapist to call me through. I always hated waiting there. It was when I felt like most like an animal. They herded us in there one by one. I hated seeing the other broken people leave the same door I had just come in, as if we were on some carousel. I wondered whether anyone ever left this place feeling fixed. *You're not broken.* I can almost feel the bloody support group shout. No, of course. We're not broken, we don't need fixing. But we do don't we. Every single person who walks in here isn't how they are supposed to be. We fucked up. We are fuck ups. And we need weekly interventions with a non-fucked up human to talk about our fuck ups endlessly to learn how not to fuck up again. And it's pretty fucking exhausting if I'm being honest.

77

"Gavin?" My therapist poked her head round the corner and I stood up and followed her into our room. Despite all of my reservations, I actually really liked her. Her name was Lesley and she was a little overweight, but the endearing kind of overweight, like she would cook you a nice dinner. She had short brown hair which framed her face and she was calm. She was always calm. When I screamed and shouted, when I broke down hysterically, when I was morbidly sarcastic, she remained calm. And that gave me peace.

"So how have you been since last week Gavin?"

"Okay I guess, just the usual bits and bobs".

"Did you end up calling your son on his birthday? I know we were discussing the possibility last week". I froze, not wanting to think back to that day, to the things that I had seen and the things I had done.

"No, I didn't, I chickened out. I know it's cowardly".

"Cowardly? What makes you say that?"

"Because I was scared. I didn't want to be ignored."

"Why? How would that feel?"

"Like shit. Like I've failed. I just don't want to hear that I've lost all chance of redemption. I need to hold on to that for a little while longer". Silence. And in that silence my mind flashed back. To the fear. To the panic. To the sounds of her screams and the sound of my own breath as I stood there in the icy cold air.

I couldn't really focus for the rest of our session but I put on a pretty good show for being 'present' because after all, we need to be '*mentally present and not just physically present to get the most out of these sessions together'.* I had learnt that pearl of wisdom pretty early on. She tried to bring up Dan again but I made clear that I was done with that conversation. *It is okay to draw boundaries. Advocating for yourself is one of the bravest things you can do.* I had been told that after I had sworn blind at her during one of our first sessions. I had paced around the room seething and swearing and balling my hands into fists ready to go. She hadn't flinched. She didn't speak. She just let me feel the anger boil over. I goaded her, willing her to yell at me, to hit me, to chuck me out at the very least. I wanted her to say I was beyond fixing. But her silence said otherwise. And her being there every session after that was more telling than any telling off. After that, I was sure she was here for the long haul.

For the rest of the hour, we touched on my job and how I was finding it. We briefly spoke about my childhood but she had learnt not to push me too hard on that. I could cope in short snippets of conversation but any longer and I exploded. I exploded in a way which was so uncomfortable to me. It wasn't the red rage I was familiar with but rather a deep aching usually characterized by an endless stream of tears that I couldn't stop. It must have been my fourteenth or fifteenth session when I first told her about those Friday afternoons with dad in the carpark. I had never told a single soul before her and I haven't told a single soul since. I remember being grateful that she didn't make me say it. It seemed that my hysterical breathing and eruption of tears had been enough to tell my story.

Lily

I undressed her slowly, taking my time to feel each curve of her body. I spent most time on her tits; each time I ran my fingers over them, I felt her surrender a little more. It was as if the gentler I caressed them, the more she quivered; the anticipation had always been half the game with her after all. I kissed down her body, feeling her smooth skin against my lips. Rubbing my tongue down the inside of her thigh, I felt her hand on the back of my head, willing me to taste her, begging me to make her scream.

And that's when I heard it. The screech. But it wasn't like I had heard before. It wasn't a scream coated in pleasure but instead one that made my blood run cold. Pulling my head up, all I could see was blood pouring from her stomach. Her hands clutching her body, fear flooding her eyes as she stared at me. "Please don't let me die", she begged.

I woke in a hot sweat, panic surging through me. Sitting bolt upright in bed, I started frantically searching, not sure what it was I was looking for. I looked up to see how she was doing but she had gone. Disappeared before my eyes. I burst into tears, relief pouring through me that it was just a dream. And then the almost instant realisation that the dream was real after all and that she was dead. The realisation that I couldn't save her and that she was gone forever.

I forced myself out from the bed and stood under a freezing cold shower, the pellets of water bruising my skin like icicles. I let the tears fall alongside the water and slowed my breathing right down until it no longer felt like my head might explode. As I wrapped myself in a huge towel when I got out from the shower, it felt like being hugged by her and I began to cry all over again. When I finally made it back to the bedroom, I lay face down on the sweat-ridden sheets and gave way for the grief to swallow me. The pain of longing for someone who is no longer there is the cruelest form of torture. It is a never-ending fall; my stomach churning as I cascade down a waterfall into pitch blackness before being hauled beneath the surface.

Gavin

The sound of a car alarm going off woke me up at 5:23am. I stood up and peered out the window, half expecting to see someone with pliers breaking in but there was no one in sight. I wondered how long it would be before the owner stopped the sound as I could feel myself becoming more and more wound up by the second. I didn't bother going back to bed. Instead, I flicked onto Netflix and started to mindlessly trawl through the endless options, hoping something half-interesting might pop up. It was Tuesday now. It had been two days since the news had broken.

The headlines about Ayla Stevens had flashed across the TV screen at 8am on Sunday. The news presenter stated that they believed she was murdered between 12am and 2am in the early hours of that morning. I couldn't believe how quickly tragic news travelled. It sounded awful. The news presenter stated that Ayla was a seventeen-year-old girl who was fatally stabbed in a park in Pembrokeshire and they were appealing for witnesses who might have seen anything suspicious to come forward. That whole day my social media had been flooded with tributes to her and her family; an endless outpouring of love and support and sadness for what they were going through. I had been transfixed by it all, religiously reading every post on her Facebook page, continuously refreshing the newsfeed on my phone to see if there had been any further updates in the case. I couldn't help but be so utterly morbidly curious. I wondered about how long it would be before they started calling people in for questioning. I wondered how long I had before I would be called in.

It was Thursday now and the news of Ayla had slowed already. There had been a school shooting in America just yesterday which had stolen the headlines. The shooter's face was plastered all over the internet and I couldn't help but feel the prick got what he wanted. News articles about Ayla could still be found but I was having to scroll further down my feed to get to them. I pulled up the most recent article and read that an eighteen-year-old man had been called in for questioning. My body froze over as I read the words.

An eighteen-year-old man has been brought in for questioning over the murder of Ayla Stevens, 17, on Saturday night. Police are

not providing the name of the man at this stage but have released
the following statement.

We are working tirelessly around the clock to uncover who
committed this heinous crime. We will not stop until justice is
served for Ayla and her family. We are still encouraging anyone
with any further information to come forward which might aid our
investigation.

My mind whirred as my brain tried to compute the words in any way which wasn't the truth. I couldn't help but think of all the vigilantes on the forums who would do everything they could to release that anonymous information out into the public. *Please God no.* After re-reading the article for the fifteenth time, I eventually prized myself away from my phone, willing myself to put an end to the self-inflicted torture. I checked my watch. 8:56am. Three hours of my life had disappeared through scrolling and I hadn't even realised it. I needed to be at work in an hour so I threw on my clothes and whacked a couple of slices of bread into the toaster. As the toast cooked, I brought back up my phone and started to doom scroll yet again. The addiction to the trauma was compelling.

I sat and ate my marmite on toast at the table listening to the radio with my phone glued to my hand the entire time. I wasn't even sure what it was that I was looking for but I knew that I hadn't yet found it. I checked the time again. 9:34am. It was time for me to go. Locking up the flat, I walked the twenty minutes down the road to my first client for the day; a couple who had recently had a baby and were clearly re-adjusting to the throws of parenthood. I rung their front door and the woman opened it looking flustered.

"Hello? Can I help you?"

"It's me, the gardener. I come once a fortnight". Embarrassment flushed across her face.

"Oh my god, I'm so sorry. I've got baby brain galore at the minute. Please do come in. What can I get you to drink? A tea? Coffee?"

"A coffee would be great thanks".

"Wonderful. How are you?" I hadn't expected to engage in conversation. Most people tended just to lead me straight into their garden.

"Yeah, I'm well thanks. Didn't get much sleep last night because a car alarm was going off from five so it was a bit of a rough start to the day". I wanted to tell her about Ayla, about the news story I had read about an eighteen-year-old being taken in for questioning. I wanted to tell her that it was my Dan and that I was frightened for him. I wanted to curl into a ball on her sofa and weep like a child.

"Oh dear, that's terrible. Well sit down and have a coffee in here before getting started then". I smiled.

"That's very kind of you, thank you". The word made me flinch as it left my mouth. *Kind.* It dawned on me that kindness was such a rarity in my life that I didn't quite know how to navigate it. I guess its existence had always made me a little uneasy.

I'm kind to you, aren't I? Dad's words echoed in my ears. I had barely nodded but he continued anyway. *We need to keep this between us Gavin. Otherwise, I won't get to be kind to you anymore. Otherwise, the kindness will have to stop.* I winced thinking about his hand caressing the top of my leg as he said it. I remember thinking how desperately I had wanted the kindness to stop.

"How's parenting going?" I asked, frantically begging my brain not to be in that moment. Anywhere but there.

"It's wonderful and exhausting and magical and hard all wrapped up into one. We're loving it". I smiled.

"Do you have any children of your own?" My mind evaporated and thoughts of Dan and Lily growing up poured down. I nodded but didn't add anything else and I'm sure she sensed my loss because she didn't ask anything further. I took a sip from my mug.

"Now that is a bloody good coffee". She smiled and I felt the energy resurface in the room.

I didn't end up telling her about the news article or about Dan and the arrest but I spent the two hours I was gardening musing on what her reaction might have been. I wondered whether she would have been sympathetic and invited me in for another cup of coffee or instead whether her brow would have furrowed and she would have quickly found an excuse for why the garden no longer needed tending to.

Hayley

It was early when they arrested Dan. It just so happened to be in
one of the snippets of time that I was awake and wasn't yet high.
I had just woken from a long and groggy sleep. The battering of
the door was so loud but Lils and Dan stayed in their rooms.
"Is Daniel Draker here?" I nodded,
"Yeah, he's just upstairs". They didn't need anything more than
that. They barged their way past me and headed straight up the
stairs and into the bedrooms as I chased after them.
"Daniel Draker, I am arresting you on suspicion of the murder of
Ayla Stevens. You do not have to say anything but it may harm
your defense if you do not mention when questioned something
which you later rely on in court. Anything you do say may be
given in evidence". I watched as his face sunk to the floor. I
wanted to scream at them. Danny wasn't there. I was the one with
her phone. Arrest me, I wanted to shout but no words escaped my
lips. Instead, I stayed silent. I didn't say anything to them and I
didn't say anything to Danny. I watched on as they stole my child
in front of my own eyes and I didn't mutter a single word.

Danny

I felt a calmness wash over me. As I was piled into the back of the
police car, I looked back to see Lily and Mum standing in the

doorway, holding each other. Maybe this could be the start of something good, I thought.

By the time I arrived at the station, the reality had well and truly sunken in. The cell was cold. I tried to control my breathing but I couldn't quite get a handle on it. My head spun and my thoughts ran and ran and ran and wouldn't fucking stop. Twenty-four hours they had. Twenty-four hours before they could either charge me or send me on my merry way. I could feel the clock begin to tick away in my head. Tick tock, tick tock. It was like music. I lay myself down on the concrete with my face towards the ceiling. There was a strange sort of peace which levitated just above me cocooning me from the fear. Tick tock, tick tock. Whatever they had, they had. Whatever they found, they found. Tick tock, tick tock. I had spent the last couple of weeks covering tracks, trying my absolute best to act like everything has been fine, like nothing had happened that night. Tick tock, tick tock. But it had, and I knew everything was about to come crashing down. Tick tock, tick tock.

I closed my eyes and I was right back there again. I saw the blood dripping down her face. I could hear her visceral scream, the sound of her footsteps running away echoed in my ears. I had always promised myself that I wouldn't end up like Dad, that I would never ever raise my fist to a woman. I had so desperately wanted to believe that I was better than that. I had so desperately not wanted to morph into him. But as I lay on the hard, cold, concrete floor, I couldn't help but think the apple didn't fall far from the tree after all. Maybe I was right where I belonged, maybe

I was destined for this all along. Just as I was started to doze off, I heard the metal door clank open.

"It's time for your interview mate, let's go". *Mate*. I felt the word pierce through me. I couldn't help but wince. Something told me this man and me would not be mates. Not in the real world and certainly not in here. It was light outside as he walked me down the corridor towards the interview room; an unwelcomed reminder of slowly the clock was ticking. I thought about how I would usually only just be getting out of bed and scoffing down some breakfast at this time. I wondered whether Lily and Mum would have gone back to sleep after they took me away. I wondered how long it would have taken before Mum shot up in the bathroom and Lily was left in her own silence. I wondered how she would be feeling now; I wondered if this had taken her back to the trauma. If the silence that remained screamed louder than the last time.

"This interview is being tape recorded and may be given in evidence if your case is brough to trial. We are in interview room 1 at Haverfordwest police station. The date is 22nd February 2024 and the time by my watch is 7:21am. I am Detective Constable Jenkins. The other police officer present is Detective Constable Mack. Please state your full name and date of birth"

"Daniel Draker. 17th February 2006"

"Before the start of this interview, I must remind you that you are entitled to free and independent legal advice either in person or by telephone at any stage. Do you wish to speak to a legal advisor now or have one present during the interview?"

"Nah, I don't want no solicitor". A few of my mates had been in trouble with the police before. One of my mate's parents had splashed out on some fancy ass solicitor and lawyer for him and he had ended up in juvie. After that had happened, the chat in the pub had been that having a solicitor had made him look guilty. I wasn't about to add to my chances of getting locked up.

"That's fine. If you change your mind, let us know and we can appoint one to you. That is your right". I nodded. *Nice fucking try,* I thought.

"Right Daniel, we all know why we're here. And we all know why it is you who is sat opposite us right now. So, I am going to see if we can save us all some time and you can just tell us exactly what happened that night".

"What night?" That was another thing my mates who had been arrested before had said was a laugh. Have a bit of fun. Wind them up. And it looked like it was working already. I could see DCI Mack picking at his fingers like he was anxious. *Pathetic,* I thought to myself. I wasn't going to make this easy for them. I suddenly felt a thrill of power in being here. There was something about it which made me feel important in a way I hadn't before.

"On the 17th February, your birthday as I understand?"

"I was at the Red Dragon, having a few beers for my birthday. Is that a crime officer?"

"No, it's not". A pause. The other bloke spoke then, "Did you see Ayla Stevens at the pub?",

I let out a long breath,

"Yes, I did. She only showed up for a bit though".

"Would you consider Ayla to be your friend then? Since she came to celebrate your birthday?" I instinctively went to shake my head but had to stop myself.

"I guess so. Look a lot of people came to the pub that night".

Mack chimed in then,

"What time did you leave the pub Daniel?"

"Around eleven I guess".

"And did you go straight home?"

"Yeah, I walked home with my sister". I could feel the air shift in the room.

"It's interesting that you say that, Daniel. Your sister said the same thing you see", he paused, "but that's not what happened is it?" I stared at him, unsure of how much to give.

"We have CCTV of your sister walking home alone that night, paired with a text message she sent you at 11:31pm. So now we know that both you and your sister are lying Daniel. And I'm sat here wondering why that might be". He paused again, allowing the immensity of his words to dance around the room for a moment or two.

"How did you feel about your sister being in a gay relationship Daniel?" The question caught me off guard. It felt so poisonous. I took a deep breath in and purposefully tried to slow my breathing. This was important. I knew I couldn't let them see the venom had reached my bloodstream already. As I did, I glanced down and noticed I was picking at my fingers. Fuck.

"Fine" I responded through baited breath.

Jenkins spoke again then,

"Tell us Daniel, did you speak to Ayla much that night?"

"Nah, not really."

"Interesting" He paused, "Did you and Ayla Stevens have any kind of alteration at the pub?"

"No, not that I can recall", I responded without flinching. There was another pause then as Jenkins started shuffling a few papers in front of him.

"When your sister Lily left the pub and walked home that night Daniel, what did you do?"

"I stayed until the pub closed and then I went to get some chicken and chips and headed home". He was getting restless; I could feel it in the silences.

"We have found discovered some quite damning evidence Daniel". He glanced over to his colleague, "Evidence which shows us you did in fact have an alteration with Ayla that night". Again, she paused and the sound of her silence was starting to get underneath my skin.

"Lying in an interview looks really bad to a jury you see Daniel. So, I'd think very carefully about the impression you want to give".

"I'm not. I did speak to her, just not for very long." I don't know why I bothered lying. But I was backed into a corner. I didn't want to give them anything until I absolutely had to.

"What did you say to her in this conversation then?"

"I told her to look after my sister".

"Imagine I'm Ayla, Daniel. Can you recall exactly what it is you said to her?" the patronizing tone of his voice grated me but I had to let it slide if I wanted to get through this.

"I told her to take good care of my sister, that was it, swear down".

"And how did Ayla respond to that Daniel?" I felt the heat rising in me as I replayed the moment over in my head. I couldn't afford to give them a possible motive. I knew full well that a girl simply poking a bear wouldn't justify her murder.

"She said Lily loved her and she loved Lily and of course she would take good care of her". I said through gritted teeth.

"How interesting". Jenkins replied. I couldn't understand what he meant. I sat still, my face expressionless. I could feel the cameras on me. It felt like twelve pairs of eyes were searing through the lens, judging my every movement.

"Daniel, we have some CCTV from outside the pub that night. I'm going to give you another chance to tell us what happened before I share that footage with you". 'Call their bluff', I could hear my mates yelling through the void. I'd heard stories of police lying about what evidence they had against you to make you admit to something.

"I've said all I need to say. That was all that happened".

"Very well. For the tape, DCI Mack is now going to play the CCTV footage – evidence 12". Twelve? What were numbers one to eleven? The heat rose in me yet again and a single droplet of sweat rolled down by right cheek.

The footage was grainy but there was no doubt who it was. Ayla was jogging and yelling. She stops and I slowly come into the lens of the camera. She's calm, collected. She has a smarmy grin pasted over her face. She always thought she was better than everyone else. I look tense, my shoulders broad. She looks tiny next to me. I could feel the moment she said it through the screen. I could see my knuckles clench into a fist,

"Are you jealous? Is that what it is? I'll tell you what. I'll scream your name when she's fucking me tonight, how about that?"

Whack. My fist made contact with her face before I had the chance to even take a breath. It was so instinctive, like there was nothing I could have done to stop it from happening. As I watched it, I was expecting regret to swarm my body like an infestation of flies but it didn't. Instead, I was greeted by a warm glow of pride. I didn't have time to think about what that said about me. DCI Mack stopped the tape and stared at me.

"Now as I see it Daniel, that's not two people having a pleasant, civil conversation about how much you both care for your sister". I took a deep breath, unsure of which direction I should now take.

"Okay look, I legit said that to Ayla. I said that I was happy for them and that I wanted to make sure she would treat Lils right. Legit, that's what I said".

Mack twisted the knife, "For arguments sake, let's say that is the case then". I hated how little he believed me; I hated the tone of his sarcastic voice.

"How could Ayla have possibly responded to make you react by punching her in the face?" I needed to tread carefully here. I didn't want them to know everything. I was caught between desperately wanting to expose Ayla for the monster she was, and protecting my carefully curated version of the truth.

"She said that I was jealous. She made out like I fancied her or some crap". Mack looked perplexed.

"And that made you angry enough to hit her?" I nodded, confusion too spreading across mine. It was as if he didn't know how little it took for me to see red. It was as if all he had ever experienced was a glowing orange, a hollowed anger which could be tempered with a few deep breaths or counting to ten.

"Yes, it did. I regret it, it was wrong".

"What happened after you hit her Daniel?"

"I went to the chicken shop and then went home, I swear down"

"I don't think that's what happened Daniel" Detective Mack quietly said, "I think you followed Ayla didn't you. I think you were so mad that you followed her and stabbed her in the park. Maybe you hadn't meant for her to die..."

"No, I didn't. I was mad with her yes but I realised that hitting her had been a mistake. I went home"

"Did you kill Ayla Stevens Daniel?"

"No". I tried to make my voice sound as stern as I could but every word I spoke sounded hollow coming from my mouth.

They led me back to the cell after that. I lay down on the cold floor, trying to calm my manic mind. I thought about what they had. A video of me punching Ayla the night of her murder, it didn't look good. But Ayla wasn't punched to death outside of the pub that night. She was stabbed in Boddington Park. Surely there wasn't enough evidence to charge me.

I was right. One of the officers came and got me from my cell what felt like hours later. He guided me to the front desk where a short woman told me that I was being released on bail and that I may have to come back in for more questioning soon. I wanted this to be done with. The idea of coming back in for more questioning was a noose around my neck. It felt like a time bomb just waiting to go off.

Lily

Dan got back at 2:30pm. I hadn't gone to school; how could I have possibly pretended that everything was fine when the most important person in my life had been arrested and I didn't know if he would be coming back. I sat in my room and stared out the window, thinking he might walk down the street at any given moment. It wasn't meant to be this way. I felt so angry at Ayla in those moments. If it wasn't for her, then none of this would be happening after all.

I closed my eyes and my mind immediately placed me back there. She was standing beside the bar; one hand elegantly poised on her hip and the other balancing on the countertop. Her hair so beautifully framed her face that I couldn't help but stare. A young guy wormed his way towards her and I watched on as they started to chat and laugh and just be. I watched on as her body language slowly shifted. I watched as her hand fell away from her hip and started to twizzle in her hair. Her eyes became animated

95

as they chatted and her huge brown eyes flitted towards a focus on his lips. The sides of her mouth rose into a wicked smile as she took half a step toward him. My stomach lurched. She bit her bottom lip.

I couldn't take it anymore. I flung my eyes open and could feel the tears streaming down my face. I hated her for tainting our last true memory together. I hated her for dying. And I hated her for having Danny arrested.

"Oh my god, you're back, thank god", I ran towards him as soon as he was through the front door. "Are you okay? What happened? Oh my god, I've been so worried". He shook off my hug.

"Yeah, all fine, don't worry about it. They've released me on bail".

"But why did they arrest you? I don't understand".

"They knew you were lying about us coming home together. There was CCTV. They'll probably want to speak to you at some point again about it". Shit. Everything felt like it was already falling to pieces. He brushed past me and started back up the stairs. I wanted to go after him but something inside me told me to leave it alone.

Hayley

I sat up in bed when I heard the door slam shut. I let out a breath I wasn't aware I had even been holding. He was home; my boy was home. I could feel the shivers run through me like a wind chill. I touched my hand to my arms and my skin felt cold to the touch. I closed my eyes, willing myself to think of anything but the beating memory that pulsated through my veins.

She lay completely still, rain pounding the ground. Her eyes were like glass, staring directly through me. I was silently begging her to blink, to give me some sign of life. I saw the stream of blood that had once been inside her circling in a pool of water and draining away with the rest of the rain. I didn't speak. I just reached my hand out and touched the side of her arm. She was like ice. My eyes frantically looked around but there was no one else there. The eerie silence stood as a stark reminder of her stillness, her emptiness. Without thinking, I rose to my feet and started to run, the striking of the ground relieving me from the grasp of her ghost I left lying dead in the mud.

I climbed out of the bed and forced myself into the shower. The water burned my skin and I hoped it might sear through and into my body, cleaning me from within. I could feel the need for another hit already begin to settle into my core, the nausea rose up within me and I began to wretch as the water poured around. The vomiting always seemed to surface out of nowhere, overhauling my body before I had a chance to swallow it down. I was grateful that it usually set in before the sadness and the guilt and the remorse. It gave me the prior warning I needed.

As I stumbled out of the shower, I caught a glimpse of myself in the mirror. I couldn't remember the last time I had looked at myself. The woman staring back looked more girl than woman. Her face was pale, like the colour didn't think it was worth staying inside. Her eyes were dull but yet somehow still captivating. I was still in there I thought, buried deeply, but still there. It was hard not to feel sad looking at my reflection. The aching truth that I was not who I had promised myself I would be, stared back.

I could hear my phone begin to buzz from my bed and as I walked towards it, I wondered who would possibly be calling me. I didn't have any friends. Tentatively, I picked up,

"Hello?"

"Hi there, is that Hayley Draker"

"Speaking?"

"It is Detective Jenkins. We would like you to come into the station for a voluntary interview tomorrow to answer some questions regarding the death of Ayla Stevens".

"Questions? About what?" My heart rate began to quicken and I tried to steady my voice, determined not to give him an inch.

"We will go through the questions tomorrow, Miss Draker. I'm sure you'll understand the gravity of the situation". He paused, "I think it's best if we speak about it face to face. Does tomorrow work for you?"

"Err, tomorrow, err yeah I guess that's fine".

"Brilliant, come down to the station for 11:15am and we'll get everything underway"

"What do you mean? I don't know what you're even talking about."

"We will go through everything tomorrow, Miss Draker. 11:15am, at the police station. See you there, thank you for your time".

The line went dead and I still held the phone up to my face, trying to filter what any of this meant. How much did they know? I wanted to cry but I couldn't find the strength. Instead, I fumbled for the dope in the little plastic bag by my bed and prepped the needle. Soon everything would be better. Soon the panic in my head would fade. Soon I wouldn't be able think anything at all.

Hayley

The kids didn't know I had been called in for questioning. I wasn't completely out of it when my alarm went off at 10am the next morning but I wasn't exactly going to win any awards for being 'mother of the year' either. I managed to scrape together a somewhat respectable outfit and slap on some old eyeliner I found lying on the floor. I couldn't tell you if I was sober if I'm honest. The pain felt like sobriety but it had been so long since I'd been clean for more than an hour that I'd forgotten what it felt like. I threw up three times before I left the house and could feel the sweat sticking to me like it was clinging on for dear life. Was I really going to be able to do this? I wasn't going to be able to do it sober, I was certain of that. Before I left the house, I took a couple of drags and breathed in deeply, hoping for the euphoria to embed itself deep inside my lungs; maybe it could cling there long enough to survive this interview.

I decided to walk to the station. It was only about twenty minutes and I thought the fresh air might do me some good. As I walked, I thought of nothing. It was the kind of emptiness that comes so rarely that it is over the moment it is acknowledged. I walked slowly, ignoring how mothers pulled their children closer toward them as I approached. I had no idea whether it was instinct or experience that caused the tug of panic or overprotective crossing of the road. I decided not to dwell on the monster they thought I was.

When I walked into the police station, I felt a wave of relief spill over me. I felt safe in here. I had been here at my most vulnerable. I had shared secrets here that I once thought would never pass my lips. This station was the first place I had ever felt heard. I thought back to the cups of tea that DCI Packer had made me before each interview and how she always made sure my water glass was full. I remember feeling an overwhelming sadness when the tape was turned off in my final interview. I remember the deafening silence in the house when I got home. I remember her calling me up on the day that he was charged and I could hear the tears rolling down her cheeks before I even felt them on mine.

"Hi, I'm here for an interview. My name is Hayley Draker". The man behind the glass peered out from behind his computer screen. "Good morning. If you could just sign this here and then take a seat on the chairs over there. DCI Jenkins will come and get you in a few minutes or so. Help yourself to a drink from the machine".

I sat down, feeling a wave of realisation wash over me. I wasn't here to talk about a man who had abused me for years. I wasn't likely to get the same comforting looks and opportunities for respite from the questions as I had been gifted all those years ago. They were going to be asking me about Ayla Stevens. I pulled my knees up towards my chest as I sat curled up in the chair. I needed to decide how much I was willing to share.

A tall, lanky man approached me a few minutes later. "DCI Jenkins" he said as he towered over me. "Are you Hayley Draker?" I nodded. All the saliva in my mouth had dried up and I felt like I couldn't get a word out.

"Please follow me", he said as he gestured towards the door. As I followed him down the corridor, it felt like the walls were closing in around me and I pictured being squished between them, flattened like a bug. I smiled at the thought. When we got to the room, it was not how I had remembered it. There was still water on the table and a tape recorder on the side, but it smelt different. It was a mixture of coffee and old cigarettes. I wanted to cry. I even more desperately wanted to feel the relief of smack flood through me. The hit I had taken from home was beginning to wear off and the sensation of nausea was once again beginning to settle into my bones. I would be home soon, I told myself. All of this would be over soon.

"The interview is being taped recorded and may be given in evidence if your case is brought to trial. We are in interview room 1 at Haverfordwest police station. The date is 23rd February 2024 and the time by my watch is 11:31am. I am Detective Constable

Jenkins. Please state your full name and date of birth". I gulped. Even the idea that this tape could be played in a courtroom one day was terrifying.

"Hayley Draker. I was born on 11th June 1984". He nodded.

"The other police officer present is Detective Constable Peters. Do you agree that there are no other persons present?"

"Yes". I couldn't recognise my own voice, it felt so detached.

"Before the start of this interview, I must remind you that you are entitled to free and independent legal advice either in person or by telephone at any stage. Do you wish to speak to a legal advisor now or have one present during the interview?"

"No". There was a pause then before Peters started talking which I hadn't been expecting.

She looked far too young to be a detective. She was tiny sat next to DCI Jenkins and had an air of someone who thought more about themselves than anyone else did.

"Hayley, do you know Ayla Stevens?" I glanced over to DCI Jenkins as if he had the power to save me from this question.

"Yes, I do. She's my daughter's friend".

"Your daughter is Lily Draker is that correct?"

"Yes".

"How long have Ayla and your daughter been friends?"

"Umm, I'm not sure to be honest. Maybe a couple of years I guess?" I felt a wave of embarrassment wash over me. I wondered what they thought of me, not knowing my own daughter's friends.

"And is this the only context in which you had any form of contact with Ayla Stevens?" I could feel the room around me start to close in and I again envisioned a flattened version of me lying across the table. The heat in my body ran through to my face.

"Y- y- yes".

"You sound unsure?"

I shook my head. There was a beat of silence before the next question.

"Do you use recreational drugs Hayley?" Scattered thoughts ran through my head. Was there really any point in lying? Surely, they would be able to prove pretty easily that I do drugs. It wouldn't take a detective to figure it out. I hated them for making me say it anyway.

"Occasionally".

"And when you 'occasionally' use drugs Hayley, who do you purchase these from?" I was making this too easy for them.

"A few different people". They nodded.

"And did one of these people happen to be Ayla Stevens?" The game was up, I thought. I didn't know how they knew but they did.

"Yes".

DCI Jenkins took over then.

"When was the last time you brought drugs from Ayla"?

"Umm I dunno. A couple of weeks ago maybe".

"Did you always pay for your drugs at the time you brought them Hayley"?

"Most of the time yes"

"Most of the time? What exactly do you mean by that? What happened when you didn't pay for your drugs?" I paused,

"Occasionally Ayla would give me a hit and I would owe her the money. I'd just pay her the next time I saw her when my money came in. It was no big deal, we both agreed to it". This time they paused, as if they were waiting for me to just tac a murder confession on to the end of my sentence. I didn't.

"And were there any times when you couldn't pay her the next time you saw her?" I stared at each of them in turn before nodding ever so slightly.

"For the tape please"

"Yes, sometimes".

"Did you owe Ayla Stevens money when she was killed Hayley?"

"Yes"

"How much?" I started to rack my brain as if I didn't already know the answer.

"Umm I dunno, about four hundred". Another pause. This time, DCI Jenkins took a sip of water but didn't break eye contact with me.

"£400 is a lot of money. How were you planning on paying that back?" None of this looked good. I knew that. I could picture the headlines now 'Junkie murders drug dealer to avoid debt'. It dawned on me that when I pictured those headlines, the worst thing I imagined was being put on a black list by other dealers. The risk of that sent shivers down my spine.

"I was looking for a job", I could hear how feeble my words sounded, like they were breaking before they had even landed. I was taken aback by the speed of the questions, the confidence in each one they asked. There didn't seem to be any hesitation, any second guessing.

"You can see how this looks Hayley can't you? Ayla Stevens dying has worked out remarkably well for you, hasn't it? £400 worth of debt wiped, just like that". I didn't respond. I didn't know what I could possibly say to make anything better.

"Did you see Ayla the day she died?" I shook my head before I even had the chance to decide what I wanted to say.

"No, I didn't. I haven't seen her for a while".

He pursed his lips, baiting me to change my mind but I stood my ground. I wished DCI Packer had been here. I needed to hear her tell me that it was all going to be okay, I needed her to reassure me that I could be honest. Again, my mind flashed back to her body lying still on the ground. I imagined the worms beginning to circle her and crawl over her lifeless body. I wondered whether I was now the monster I had always claimed not to be. How many mistakes does someone have to make before it becomes a choice?

"Where were you between 12am and 2am on Saturday 17th February 2024 Hayley?"

"I was at home in bed". I responded with a confidence I certainly didn't feel.

"Would anyone be able to verify that you were at home at this time?" I paused.

"I'm not sure. I don't know when Lily and Dan got back from the pub that night" I paused, "But I was in my room anyway".

"So, you aren't able to clarify whether Lily or Daniel were at home at that time either then? You don't remember hearing them come into the house?"

"No. I was most likely asleep at that time, I'm a heavy sleeper".

"Did you murder Ayla Stevens, Hayley?" The question shot through the air like a dagger, catching me off guard.

"No, I didn't. I promise you I didn't" I could hear the sound of desperation in my voice and I wondered how it vibrated across the room; did the echo sound like guilt or innocence? DCI Jenkins stared at me, tapping his pen against the table.

"A seventeen-year-old girl has lost her life Hayley," he paused as if it were another question for me to answer,

"Her parents will never be the same again. We owe it to them to bring her killer to justice". I nodded.

"If you are hiding anything Hayley, we will find out. I urge you to think about that poor girl's parents", again he paused, waiting for me to fill in the unbearable silence.

"I don't know anything". I could feel the world around me closing in and I hoped it might swallow me up and take me away from this place, from this moment.

"We will have to take your word for it for now. We will be taking your phone in for examination as we believe it may aid our investigation. We will be in touch soon for further interviews I'm sure". I nodded.

"This interview is finished at 12:49pm", he said as he tapped the tape recorder and stood up. I felt like I could finally breathe and I noticed the nausea return with that very same breath. I knew that

106

this wouldn't be the end of this saga and I knew that I would have more to answer for. But for now, it was over. And the next thing I could do was get my fix. As I walked out of the interview room, the prospect of that was all I could think about.

The rain started to pour as soon as I left the station like I was in some fucking film. Only in the film, you're meant to feel somewhat sorry for the damsel-caught-in-the-rain and I couldn't help but think no one in their right mind would muster any sympathy for me. As I walked back home and felt the rain hitting against my body as the wind howled in my face, I imagined her body lying there. I pictured her arms covered in goosebumps, her teeth chattering from the chill. I felt a rare maternal urge to give her a blanket. I knew that her body would have been moved by now and that she would be warm and safe in a morgue somewhere but I couldn't picture it anywhere but the rotting ground. *She's safe and warm, she's okay,* I told myself. I guess, that is, if you can feel warm and safe once you're already dead.

Danny

I woke up to the sound of the alarm ringing in my ear. Friday. I couldn't believe quite how quickly my world could fall apart. I stared gormlessly at my phone as I lay in bed. A string of endless messages still pinging through. I had ignored all of the questions and incessant messages I had been getting from my mates. I had also ignored all of the questions and incessant messages I had been getting from people who definitely *weren't* my mates for that matter too. People who I hadn't spoken to in months or even years had suddenly crawled out from the woodwork to offer their condolences and 'check in' on how I was coping. I wanted to tell them how I barely even knew the girl for god's sake and that I didn't exactly need cheering up. But then these people weren't really looking to offer comfort anyway. Most of these pricks couldn't care less how I was *actually* doing. They just were seeking the thrill of it all; the opportunity to say that they had the inside scoop. Tragedy doesn't bring people together; it doesn't unite people amongst the sadness. Instead, it felt like any 'unity' was driven by an innate selfishness, an inhumanely human desire to win.

I pulled myself up from the comfort of my bed and threw on some clothes. I desperately didn't want to go to school but I knew I had to make it look like everything was normal. I knew how I would be scrutinized by everyone for simply being there that night. I could imagine how it looked. I'd never exactly tried that hard to hide how much I had hated Ayla so I was sure the rumour mill would be going wild. As I walked through the school gates, she was still all anyone was talking about. It was a virus spreading like wildfire, becoming more dangerous at every turn. Kieran was chatting shit about some older guys jumping her and stealing all her gear. Vicky swore blind that Ayla had faked the whole thing and fled to another country to start over. And little Roy claimed he had brought the knife and helped to bury the body. It was school stuff you know. It was children trying their best to make sense of a situation they ought never to have been in in the first place. Because even the people who never knew Ayla, they too would carry this with them wherever they now went. This would never leave their bones. Somewhere deep in their psyche, this trauma would burrow itself. And for most, it was bound never to surface again. It may even be forgotten. But for some, it would worm and weave its way into the most unsuspecting parts of their lives. It may pop its head in times of darkness or loss. It may forge their belief in a god, or more likely, their lack of belief. And for the very unfortunate few, myself most likely included, it would forge itself into every aspect of who we are; an unshakeable trauma molding us into people we were never meant to be.

"You alright mate?" a hand on my shoulder jolted me. I swung around urgently and felt a wave of relief when I saw his face. It was Ben. Ben had been my mate since primary school and although our circles drifted in and out, we had always stayed close. He was one of the bright ones. I think he was one of my only friends who hadn't cloaked themselves in hatred just because it had been easier that way. He had lost a lot of friends because of that but I had always respected him for it, from a safe distance when it was needed of course. You don't exactly get an easy ride when you speak up for the oppressed and the bullied, at least, not in school you don't.

"Yeah, yeah I'm fine".

Ben grabbed me by the shoulders and shook me back and forth,

"Don't try that bullcrap with me Danny boy. Let's get outta here, looks like you could use a beer". I nodded and let a wry smile escape from the side of my mouth.

"The red dragon or the willow?

"Definitely the willow" I responded. When we arrived at the pub, Ben brought us a couple of pints and I pitched up at a table in the corner.

"So, mate, what's going on with you? How are you holding up since this whole Ayla thing? I can't imagine it's been easy". There was a sincerity to his question which felt alien.

"I dunno man, it's just all people are talking about. It's just a bit grating that's all". He looked suspiciously towards me and then narrowed his eyes ever so slightly.

"I know about Lily man". I froze, and felt fear creep into my bones. I stared him out. I needed him to say more, I needed to know what he meant.

"I know she's into girls and that. I know she's gay. And I know about her and Ayla". I let out a breath. I had never heard someone say that the word gay before without it being enveloped with a hush-ness or loaded as an insult. I immediately wanted to deny it, to tell him to fuck off but I didn't.

"Yeah, and what about it?" I heard myself respond before I had the chance to think.

"I just imagine she's taking all of this pretty badly and I imagine that's not so easy for you as well".

"Nah man, it's fine. She'll get over it soon enough". I took a long swig of my drink and I noticed he did the same. I thought about

110

what must be going through his head. I wondered how perfectly detached he must be from the whole thing and how peaceful that would feel. Envy buried me in those moments.

"Alright man, well look you know where I am". He tapped the top of my glass with the bottom of his as he poured the final drops into his mouth. I nodded but couldn't find any words to respond with.

"So anyway, have you seen how much Casemiro has gone for? Mad money man, mad money. Man city are a shoe in for the premiership this year, just watch". And just like that, we were onto football and girls and how much of a wanker Mr. Sallsbury had been. And in those seemingly meaningless moments, I realised why we had been friends for quite so long.

Lily

It had been a week since Danny's birthday and that night that had changed everything. Today was the day of Ayla's funeral. I woke up at 5am. I threw up. I had a cold shower and then I threw up again. I cried for an hour and then I laughed watching videos of a dog playing the piano. I threw up one more time before getting dressed and doing my makeup. The idea of seeing her family made me not want to go. I didn't know if they knew about me and I didn't want to find out. I'm sure they wouldn't want me there. I found a black dress that I had in the back of my cupboard and stared at myself in the mirror. I didn't recognise myself, not really.

The girl in the mirror looked so broken, so fragile and weak. I heard a knock at the door and Dan's face appeared around the corner. I felt a flush of embarrassment as he stared at me.

"You look nice", he stated, almost matter-of-factly.

"Thank you. It's Ayla's funeral today." I trailed off as I noticed his expression change and I felt shame cloak my body.

"It's good that you're going. It's important". He smiled, reassuringly and I let out a breath I wasn't aware I had even been holding. I gave him a grateful nod and sauntered past him, down the stairs and out the front door.

The church was only a short walk from home. Everyone piled inside and sang hymns which Ayla would have hated. Her parents read some passages from the Bible which Ayla would have laughed at. And everyone lit candles and spoke about her potential and how a life had been taken too soon. It was true what they were saying. Ayla did have potential. She was incredibly bright, painstakingly beautiful and had a way with people. Had she wanted it, the world could have been her playground. She could have had it all. But I couldn't help but think that her future wouldn't have played out that way. I more likely saw her either becoming a junkie or being behind bars by her mid-twenties. That's certainly the way it was headed when she died anyway. But I guess when someone dies young, you no longer need to think about the probability that her life would have, in reality, amounted to very little. When someone dies young, you can instead live in the fantasy of 'potential'.

At the wake I stood in the corner, trying not to catch eyes with people. My friend Paula had come with me. She had been one of my only friends who had known about Ayla when we were together. I couldn't say she approved but she knew. It wasn't that she really cared about me being gay, but she had made no secret that she didn't trust Ayla. She had described her as a wrong 'un and she had been worried that she might lead me down the wrong path. Still, I had begged her to come today so that I would have someone to stand with. I had gone back and forth over whether I should come all week. My teacher's had kept on asking me when it was, like that was the only thing they had known how to say in the days afterwards. I wondered what they would say now that it was over. I wondered how long it would be before the sympathy petered out. They had all said how the funeral would be a chance for me to say goodbye. A proper goodbye. That's what everyone kept on banging on about, saying how important it was. But I couldn't help but wonder who it was important for. It certainly wasn't for Ayla. She was dead after all.

Amongst the crowds chattering in the church hall, I saw her dad begin to worm his way across the room and I prayed that he wasn't coming to approach us. But I could feel his body striding up towards us despite the fact that I was staring at the ground in an attempt to avoid any eye contact whatsoever.

"Lily, is it?" I looked up just long enough to see that he was smiling and holding out his hand for me to shake.

"Yes, it is. I am so sorry for your loss". This was something I had learnt to say just from the twenty minutes I had been stood hiding in the corner of the room, eavesdropping on various hushed conversations. The words tasted of insincerity as soon as they left my mouth. Loss felt far too trivial; as if someone had lost a football match or misplaced their phone. This wasn't a loss. This was the birth of a grief which would never fade. This was the beginning of a father's life without his daughter. There were no words that would ever comfort the intensity of pain that he felt.

"She loved you, you know". I froze. My stomach lurched and I thought I might be sick again. This wasn't part of the disingenuous conversations I had heard. I didn't know how to respond to it.

"She told us all about you. But you know what with Alison and your dad, we understood why you wouldn't want to come over". The saliva in my mouth had dried up. What was he talking about?

"I'm sorry, what do you mean?" This time I could see him freeze, the fear in his eyes as they darted from side to side, desperately looking for a way out.

"Oh my god, I'm sorry, I thought you knew. I assumed that's why you hadn't wanted to meet us. That's what Ayla had told us".

"Knew what?" I could feel my voice becoming more frantic as I tried to piece everything together without having any of the pieces to begin with.

"Alison, my wife, Ayla's mother. Well, she was the judge who sentenced your father. I really am so sorry to break the news to you here, I really thought you knew". I couldn't speak. I couldn't hear. He murmured another apology and walked away. I could feel my legs begin to crumble and Paula held me under my arms to stop me from falling.

"I need to leave", I managed to force out.

Paula helped me into my bed and I curled into a ball, rocking myself back and forth.

"Oh my god, oh my god, oh my god" was all I could hear Paula saying on repeat, her feet pacing the ground as she did. I couldn't place it altogether in my head. Why hadn't Ayla told me any of that? Why had she told her parents that I already knew? And why couldn't I shake this sinking feeling that things might have been different had I known?

I told Paula to leave. I needed to be alone. She had insisted staying but I said I was fine and that I just needed to sleep. When she finally left, I closed my eyes and flashbacked to that night.

I had left the pub crying, feeling rage pour out of me and feeling let down that it was showing itself as sadness. I wasn't sad. I was mad. I was done with feeling like some sort of dirty secret. One moment she was fucking me in the bathroom and the next she was flirting with some bloke at the bar. For the first time in the years we had been together, I feel like I finally saw her for who she truly was. She was using me. She didn't love me like I loved her and whatever it was that we were, it certainly wasn't something I wanted.

I walked home and clambered into bed, tears still pouring from my eyes. I was finished. I wanted out. All of the anger and frustration circled and surged around inside me like a storm waiting to break. I was so intoxicated by the rage I felt. I lay in bed, eyes wide, staring up at the ceiling, adrenaline racing through my veins. As I lay in the darkness, I could feel the energy dissipate out from me in a steady, monotonous glow. My eyelids grew heavy and my heartrate slowed. Just as I was dozing off, I heard my phone ring. It startled me from my slumber. I picked up the phone and I could hear the panic in her voice before I could hear the words.

"You need to meet me. Our place. Five minutes Lily. It's important. I have to tell you something". She hung up before I had the chance to ask her anything. I didn't even wait a beat. Immediately, I jumped out of the bed and threw on my clothes without a second thought. I quickly scurried down the stairs and out of the front door into the cold night air.

She was there when I arrived. She had her phone torch on and I tentatively walked toward her. As I got closer, I could make out the bruising beneath her right eye. It looked so raw. I started to run towards her, raising my voice as I did.

"Oh my god Ayla, are you okay? What happened?" Her eyes turned dark as she told me.

"Your fucking brother did this to me Lily". Her words shot through me like daggers, turning my whole world upside down. I silently begged her to stop, to tell me she had made a mistake and that none of it was true but she didn't. I think a part of her loved what was happening; I think she loved the anguish she could see painted all over my face.

I should have walked away then. I should have given her a hug and told her that I was sorry and walked her back home. I should have even chosen then to break up with her, to gently tell her that it wasn't meant to be and that I wished nothing but the best for her. I should have had the strength to pass on her advances but I didn't. I could feel how much she needed me in those moments and I craved to be the person to soothe her through the pain. The feeling of her lips against my neck quelled the angst inside me. As I felt her tongue begin to make shapes against my skin, my knees went weak with longing. Before I knew it, she was leading me through the brambles, our fingers entwined as I followed her footsteps. She leaned forward to kiss me and I surrendered. She started to move her lips down my neck and I could feel her fingers delicately trace down the inside of my thigh, dripping as she did. I could feel the rage surge and swill around again whilst the emptiness swallowed me whole. I felt so weak, painfully aware of the control she had over me. Less than an hour ago, I had been determined to finish it all with her and yet here I was, craving to please her in any which way I could.

It was then when I caught a flash of shadows behind the tree. I had chosen to ignore it at the time, convinced myself it was my mind playing tricks. But now, as I sat on my bed in my quietened room, it all came flooding back. I knew that silhouette. But it couldn't be. I hadn't seen him for ten years. Why would he be here? In these woods? Tonight? But it was him. I knew it was. It was dad.

I didn't want to remember it. I opened my eyes, wishing it away. Why was he there that night? Why was he hiding in the forest? It all felt too much. I wanted to call him and to hear him say it wasn't true, that I was imagining all of it. But I didn't even know his number. I hadn't spoken to him in years. All of the pieces of that night smashed and collided together in the most magnificent mess. It felt like I finally had all of the pieces of the puzzle but I just couldn't seem to fit them together.

Hayley

The slam of Lily's bedroom door startled me. I was laying on my stomach and lifted my head just high enough to take a swig of water. My mouth was so dry. Flipping myself over, I lay still, staring at the celling and thinking about what Lily must be going through. An encapsulating desire to hug her overcame me; a fleeting feeling of maternal instinct. Forcing myself up from the bed, I stumbled down the stairs and made my way into the small kitchen. I grabbed a knife and chopping board and started to cut up some onions and peppers before I had the chance to stop.

"Danny, help me lay the table, will you?" I yelled upstairs. I heard the clunking of his footsteps on the stairs and felt butterflies swirl inside me. As he poked his head round the kitchen door, I anticipated his shock.

"What's going on? What are you doing?" He didn't sound angry but his words were cutting, a reminder of the mother that I had failed to be.

"I'm cooking us dinner, love. I feel like Lily could use with some TLC tonight". Danny was tall, big. When on earth did he get so big? He looked like he could crush me if he wanted to. His hair

118

was flopped over his head and he stunk of aftershave. How had I never noticed that stench before?

"Mum, I think this will just freak her out even more. I mean when was the last time we all sat down and ate dinner together? Let alone a dinner you cooked?" Maybe he could see the sadness in my eyes or maybe he just didn't want to hear me say that it hadn't been long after dad had left. A night which was etched into all of our memories like a scar that hurt more every time you looked at it.

"But yeah, I guess I'll lay the table. It's the thought that counts, eh?"

As I waited for the chicken to brown, I thought back to our first dinner together after Gavin had gone. I thought about how small Dan and Lils had been then.

"I think this could be the start of something good", Danny had said to break the deafening silence as we sat there eating. I was in awe of him in that moment. How could he be so brave? Lily had looked over to him as if she was thinking the same.

"You know what Dan, I think you could be right", I had replied. I marveled at the idea that that night could have been the start of something good, finally. I wished with everything inside me that I could have just let it be.

I felt a single tear trickle down my face. Maybe this, maybe tonight. Maybe this could be the start of something good, I thought. I heard the door open and slam shut and glanced up to Lily was standing in the doorway of the kitchen.

"What the hell is going on?" She looked around and I could feel the spite in her eyes melt into everything she locked eyes on.

"I thought it would be nice to have dinner together and-"

"Oh, for fucks sake mum really? You thought that a nice dinner might fix the last ten fucking years?"

"No, I don't Lily, but I thought it might be a good start. And especially after today, I thought you might appreciate it".

"Why after today?" Her words were venomous. She paused. Waiting, willing for me to say the wrong thing.

"Well, I know the funeral of your friend can't have been-"

"My friend?" And there it was. The wrong thing.

"She wasn't my friend mum. We were fucking okay. We weren't 'friends'. I don't know what the fuck we were but it sure as hell wasn't that". Another pause.

"And now she's dead. So that's that I guess". I desperately wanted to say the right thing. I racked my brain for what it could possibly be but it wasn't there. I guess there never is a right thing to say with death. So instead, I said nothing. And that nothingness was the worst of all.

"So, no mum, I don't want to sit down and have dinner. After all, I wouldn't want you to miss your fix on account of all of this".

"Oi, leave it out", Danny reappeared then. His big-ness seemed more comforting than threatening now.

"Look I get you've had a shitty day, but she's trying to help. So, for god's sake, let her at least try". I glanced over to him and then back to Lils. She didn't say anything. She just shook her head and walked off, the sound of her footsteps pounding on the stairs.

Danny walked over and I felt his hands on my shoulders. "How can I help?" I felt the tears surge inside me but I was determined not to let them out.

"No, no, you're all good. It will be ready in about ten minutes. You go watch telly and I'll give you a shout when it's ready".

Lily was right. Nothing I did could fix the last ten years. I hadn't been there when she needed me the most. And I understood her apprehension now. Every few months or so I would usually make a gesture like this. I would tidy the house or cook dinner or try to hug them when they came home from school. It would usually be followed by a long speech about how I was going to quit, how I was going to get help and how sorry I was for what I had put them through. The first couple of times they believed me. The first couple of times, hell I believed myself. But then the cycle repeats and repeats and even I started to lose faith in what I was saying. I was too weak to beat this thing on my own and we were too poor to be able to afford rehab. The privilege of recovery is sadly one we can't actually afford.

When Danny and I sat down for dinner that night, I had to stop myself from starting the speech all over again. I knew how meaningless my empty promises were now. Instead, I decided not to promise anything. I decided to instead just be in that moment, with him.

"How was your day, Dan? Did you go to the funeral?"

He shook his head.

"No, I decided not to in the end. I barely knew her".

"Yeah, I guess Lily is taking it all pretty hard".

121

"She'll get over it. She just needs a bit of time and then she'll move on".

I nodded, but the tension had changed. There was a feeling I couldn't shake, a knot in my stomach. Had it come from me or from him, I wondered.

I wanted to tell him how I had a sixteen-year-old as my drug dealer. I wanted to confess about the money I owed. I wanted to tell the truth about all of the threats I had made to her, all the times I had wished her dead. But most of all, I wanted to tell him about what had happened that night. I needed to get it off my chest.

Lily

The guilt lulled before I had even reached the top of the stairs. I didn't have the energy to feel guilty or worried about Mum, I had no bandwidth to be anything but selfish tonight. As I crawled back into bed, I grabbed my pillow and clutched my arms around it, hugging it tightly. I tried to block the tidal wave of sorrow which sucked me in and spat me back out. I couldn't afford to start missing her now. I wasn't ready to admit to the enormity of the situation. I wasn't ready to accept that she was never coming back. Missing her engulfed me in those moments and the pain etched so deeply into my soul that I was sure I would be broken forever. I let the grief squeeze and twist the inside of my being for hours as I lay in bed. At least, I think it was grief but I couldn't be sure.

There were so many feelings jumbling around inside of me that I could no longer separate one from the other.

The words from the funeral still rung in my ears. I knew how Dad had felt about me being with a girl. I could imagine the rage he felt as he saw mine and Ayla's bodies entwined together that night in the woods. The memory of my one and only visit to him in prison quietly roared.

It had been a cold, crisp, November morning and I had bunked off school. I was fifteen and Ayla and I had been seeing each other for a couple of months by this point. I had sat on the bus for forty-two minutes. I couldn't believe how close the prison was to my life. How was dad so close and yet so far away? I had wondered whether he had ever been able to hear my bus journey from his cell. I hadn't told anyone that I was going. I guess I didn't want to be held accountable if I changed my mind at the last minute. I knew Mum and Danny wouldn't approve and I think most of my friends would have had too many questions. Whilst it wasn't exactly uncommon for your dad to be in prison among the people I went to school with, it was unusual among my friends. I didn't want to feel like an exciting twist in a movie or to become a fun anecdote that they could share and laugh about. I needed this to be something I was doing for me.

I remember the bus pulling up and then making the thirteen-minute walk to the gates. That was the time I considered turning back around. Did I really want to see him? I knew he wouldn't want to see me. So, was it worth the turmoil? I think deep down, I had craved to feel some sort of pain, some kind of anguish. It was difficult to explain but I had always felt that was something I had missed out on to some extent. Mum and Danny both had that with him. They both had that visceral connection with him and for whatever reason, I hadn't been worth it. I wanted to know why. They had always been wanted by Dad, albeit in a twisted kind of way. But still, I had always felt like I had missed out on that. I was never wanted.

I went through the security measures and pictured them knocking on his door and telling him he had a visitor. I felt my gut lurch when I considered that I would be the last person on his list he wanted to see. It only took eighteen minutes for him to walk through the door on the other side of the glass. I guess he wasn't that busy inside after all. He smiled and I smiled back. He looked like a different man to the one who had been taken away in handcuffs all those years ago. He had a grown a beard for one thing. And the sharp anger in his eyes had diluted into a steady glow of self-pity. He had lost weight but he didn't look weak. I could feel a knot in my stomach start to take hold as he sat down in the chair behind the glass.

"What are you doing here kiddo?" I paused. He recognised me. A wave of relief washed over me; a fear I didn't even know I had was squashed. His voice sounded hoarse, as if he had been smoking.

"I wanted to check you were okay" He laughed but the sound sent shivers down my spine. I knew Dad didn't find things funny.

"Yeah, I'm ace, how are you? How's your Mum and Dan?" I wish he knew how deeply the second half of that question cut me.

"I'm good. They're fine". Another pause, but this one felt more uncomfortable than the last.

"Don't look so glum Lil, it's me that's locked up". I could feel the anger bubbling but I pushed it back down.

"Tell me what's new with you anyway. You doing well in school? You got a boyfriend? You happy?"

"School is fine, I like science".

"Oh yeah, that's good, you're a smart cookie. I hope you don't let anyone push you about. Stay proud yeah" I couldn't help but smile at the irony of his words.

"And the boyfriend then? He better treat you right".

"Girlfriend. Her name is Ayla and she's amazing. She alw-". He pushed his chair up. He didn't look at me. He turned before I could even see the expression on his face. And just like that he was gone. I could feel the pain I had so desperately craved pour through me but it didn't feel like I had imagined it would. The conflicting emotions running through my head were enough to bury me. I had wanted anger. I had wanted love. I had wanted screaming disgust or whispered acceptance. *I had just wanted something real.*

I stared into the abyss which was left behind in fragmented pieces. My eyes turned to glass and I gormlessly stared into nothing wishing to be anywhere but there. After a few minutes, the guard gently tapped my shoulder,

"Miss? Miss?" I swiveled my head to look round to him but couldn't find the words to respond.

"Shall I see you out miss?" I nodded, shamefully pulling myself out of the chair and walking by his side back through security and out of the prison walls.

The cold wind shook me back and I wiped my face even though I was sure I hadn't cried any tears. I hopped back on the bus and watched out the window as the world passed me by faster than I would have liked.

Lying in bed, the memory seared into the back of the brain and I wondered how he would have reacted to seeing us, together, fucking amongst the trees. I wondered whether he would have just turned and walked away like he did that day in prison. Or whether he had snapped.

Gavin

My interview was on a Monday. I had to miss the morning of work which I had explained would be problematic. They had come back and said they could talk to my employer for me if it would be an issue but I would lose my job in a heartbeat if they had done that and I think they knew as much. To be honest, I think I had got a little cocky over the whole thing. It had been a couple of weeks now since Ayla had been killed and I thought they would have called me in sooner if they had suspected anything. As I sat down in the chair in the interview room, memories flooded back of the last time I had been there. I wondered whether the same fate awaited me at the other end.

"This interview is being tape recorded and may be given in evidence if your case is brought to trial. We are in interview room 3 at Cardiff Bay police station. The date is 1st March 2024 and the time by my watch is 10:18am. I am Detective Constable Scott. The other police officer present is Detective Constable Stevens. Please state your full name and date of birth".

"Gavin Draker. 9th September 1979".

"Also present is solicitor Sylvia Keynes. Do you agree that there are no other persons present"

"Yes"

Detective Scott must have been in his mid-forties. He was a big lad with broad shoulders and a balding head. His voice was gruff and he gave off the air of someone who was very sure of themselves. I had always been so envious of people who were comfortable in their own skin. It was never something which had come naturally to me and I instead endlessly jumped from one skin to the next, trying it on just long enough not to get caught out.

"Gavin, do you know who Alison Stevens is?" I had been preparing myself for the set of questions that they might ask but that opener had completely flawed me. No wonder he was so sure of himself.

"Rings a bell yeah". Sylvia had been crystal with me before we went in. This should be a no comment interview. She reminded me that a 'voluntary interview' is just a way for police to gather more information, it doesn't mean they have none. She had seen plenty of voluntary interviewees get arrested when they had opened their mouths and said the wrong thing. But I didn't like Sylvia. She seemed weak, too soft.

"How do you know Alison Stevens?"

"Not sure…is she a celebrity or something?" I smiled up at Detective Scott. This was like foreplay to me and I was just getting him warmed up. I would not be the one getting fucked at the end.

"We have been in touch with the prison officers from Highgate and they informed us that you spoke about Alison Stevens regularly during your stint there. Is this correct?" Fucking rats, I thought to myself.

"I guess I must have then. Remind me what she's been on before?" He looked pissed off now and I was getting a semi from his irritation.

"I think you know full well who she is Gavin but for the sake of the tape, Allison Stevens is the judge who sentenced you for your previous time in prison". I nodded exaggeratedly.

"Ah yes, I remember now. I guess I was just filtering what had happened to me. I was trying to make sense of it all". He looked me directly in the eye and I felt the energy change in him. He wasn't the kind of man to sit back and take it.

"Our sources tell us that you had a lot to say about Alison Stevens, Gavin. We were told that you often spoke about her in a derogatory manner. One guard said that you- "he looked down and read off the notes in front of him,

"And I quote, saw red and wanted to kill her. He said you regularly referred to her as 'the bitch who ruined my life'. Is this correct?" Before I had the chance to respond, Sylvia butted in,

"Can I remind my client of my advice to respond no comment" I barely glanced over to her before carrying on.

"I didn't like her no. I don't think you'd like the person who sentenced you to fifteen years inside either".

"Didn't like her," he paused, glancing over to DCI Jones. "Another officer told us that you said, and I quote, I am going to rape that whore in front of her kid, you'll see. Then she will know who's really in control". He paused. "It seems you felt more strongly towards Allison Stevens than just a mere dislike as you put it". It wasn't a question but he looked up at me as if waiting for a response.

"I'm guessing you've never been in prison Detective Scott. You have to spout a whole lot of shit you don't believe to get by. Everyone speaks like that. It's just what you do. It doesn't mean anything". He didn't look convinced but that was the line I was going to stand by.

Detective Stevens spoke next. She hadn't said anything yet and I had been wondering how new she was to all of this. She didn't look like a copper. She was a woman in, I would have guessed, her early thirties. She had short, black, curly hair which framed her face. She was good-looking. Her eyes were wide and her nose was slightly too big for her face, but not in an ugly way.

"Alison's daughter was murdered a couple of weeks ago. Her name was Ayla Stevens and she was just seventeen years old".

"I know," they looked back over to each other again, clearly surprised at what I had admitted. I felt Detective Stevens brain recalibrating the next question with this in mind. She was definitely new to this.

"How did you know she was dead Gavin?"

"I read the news" I replied in a sarcastic, what-a-stupid-question kind of way.

"Where were you on the 17th February Gavin?" I loved this part of an interview, the anticipation in their voices was palpable.

"You think I had something to do with her murder?" wasn't the response they had been hoping for.

"Please answer the question, Gavin. Where were you?" I took a swig of the water, biding my time. It was a thrill, toying with them.

"I was in Pembrokeshire. I went down for the day."

"Why?"

"Because it was my son's birthday and I wanted to see him". There was a pause then and I noticed DCI Stevens open and close her mouth before Detective Scott continued.

"You didn't get the train back to Cardiff that you had originally booked. Why was that, Gavin?" They had more on me than I had realised and it crossed my mind whether I should have listened to Sylvia's advice after all.

"Did you see your son on the 17th February?" I shook my head.

"No. I decided not to in the end. And I didn't get the train I had planned to get because I wanted to hang out there a bit longer. Is that a crime?" He looked me up and down.

"It's all just a bit strange you see Gavin. You haven't been to visit your children in what, ten years? And then on the day you decide to do so, the daughter of a woman you openly expressed seeking revenge on, gets murdered". Another pause. "And let's not forget that this girl was your daughter's girlfriend". He glanced up at me to seek my reaction.

"How do you feel about your daughter being in a homosexual relationship Gavin?" I stayed silent. "Is it a relationship you approve of?" I could feel the burning of both sets of eyes on me as sweat began to trickle down from my forehead. "Gavin?"

"Fine" was just about as much as I could muster. Please don't press me, I silently begged in my head.

"You don't seem particularly fine". Detective Stevens piped up.

"It's fine", I repeated and I saw Detective Scott glance towards Stevens. I think they knew I was on the edge of no comment so they parked it for now and I felt grateful for the respite.

The interview went on for another thirty minutes or so. The questions and answers quickly became repetitive, asking me why I had decided to go to Pembrokeshire and if I had told anyone I was going and why I hadn't warned Danny that I was coming to see him. They had reached a sticking point. We both knew the evidence was all too circumstantial to be accepted by the CPS for a trial just yet.

As I left the station and hopped on the bus back to my flat, I thought back to the day I had been released from prison. It had been so unremarkable that it had become so memorable as a result. I had been given back my clothes and walked out the front doors

131

like nothing had happened, as if the last eight years of my life had been erased. It was strange leaving with no one to go to home to. All of my mates on the inside had someone who would meet them when and if that release day came. But I had spent years squeezing my relationships so dry that I knew that no one would be coming for me and I had made my peace with that. All my friendships had purely been moulded around the pub. They had never been anything more than getting blind drunk and making stupid decisions. I hadn't spoken to my parents for over fifteen years by the time I was arrested. Mum had never understood why my relationship with Dad was so strained and she had never once asked. Deep down, I think she must have known. But she had buried her head so deeply underneath the sand, I doubt she'd ever come up to breathe. And so, when Dad stopped inviting me to family events, most likely worried about what secrets would be revealed in my drunken slurs, she hadn't protested. As I walked out of the prison gates, I didn't feel sad that I had no one there to greet me but instead an undeniable sense of peace.

I so vividly remember walking to the shops and buying my first beer. I remember letting myself into the flat and sitting in a heap surrounded by my few belongings; a mattress, a bottle opener with a woman with massive knockers and a huge smile plastered across her face, my laptop, and a few bags of clothes. I looked around at my life and had started to laugh. I can still feel it now. True, genuine, belly laughter. It wrapped me up so tightly that I had been sure I was going mad. Before long, the laughter had turned hysterical and tears were pouring from my face; elation and fear fused into one as I downed bottle after bottle of beer. Seventeen bottles later, I opened up my laptop and begun frantically searching.

Gavin Draker GBH court case. There were a few entries that popped up immediately, from low profile local newspapers back from 2013. I obsessively scrolled through the articles. *Judge Stevens sentences Gavin Draker to eight years in prison with no chance of parole. Judge Stevens described Mr Draker as 'a cold, calculated and manipulative man who poses a danger to society. He has shown no remorse for his actions'.* I could feel the anger bubbling away at the pit of my stomach, swirling around with the stench of the beer. I jumped onto Facebook and had quickly found Alison's profile. It hadn't taken me very long after that to find out she had a daughter. *Ayla Stevens.* The name rung in my ears and I kept flashing back to the time last year that Lily has visited me. *Ayla.* I could feel the imbalance setting in, my center of gravity being pulled off course and I wished I could have stopped myself from digging any further. It was that very first night after leaving prison that I had slotted all of the pieces together. It was from that very first night that I had a vendetta against not only Alison but now Ayla too.

Gavin

The day after the interview, I was back at work when the call came through. The number came up as unknown but I recognised Lily's voice almost instantly as I picked up the phone. Her voice had always reminded me of honey, smooth and sweet. I walked out of the garden and started pacing down the road, clinging to every word she said, just so relieved to hear her, despite the circumstances. She didn't wait long before the accusation landed, questioning my whereabouts on that fateful night just a few weeks ago. I feigned ignorance, explaining that I didn't even live in Pembrokeshire, that I couldn't have been there. I could feel her patience waning and I could hear her voice beginning to melt away. I was so desperate for her to stay with me that I didn't even care what she saying, I just needed her not to go. I wanted to beg. "I'm sorry things are so hard" I forced out before she could hang up,

"Dad, I just need to know if you were there. Honestly". I let the silence linger, "Because I need to know what you might have seen". This time I let the silence linger a little too long.

"Whatever, I've got to go," and there it was. The elongated beep that told me she was gone, yet again.

I didn't head straight back to the house after that. Instead, I strolled up to the corner shop at the end of the road and brought a packet of fags and a can of monster. Perching on the edge of the curb, I lit one of the cigarettes and inhaled deeply, feeling the smoke swirl and flutter inside my throat before breathing it back out and watching it dissipate back into the cold spring air. I pondered on whether I should have been honest with her, if only to make the conversation last that little bit longer. But it seemed wrong, given what I had seen. I had played such a little part in her life and to admit to seeing what I had, felt dirty somehow. I'm sure the guilt she felt for what she had done would eat her alive, she needn't have me as a witness to that. Not when she had never been a witness to mine.

I took a little while longer perched on the edge of the pavement, watching the world go by and wishing that I could travel along like the wind, a passenger to the anguish I had curated through bad decisions over and over again. There were so many moments in my life where I could have chosen a different path for myself. I'm not saying I could have ended up as a millionaire living in Dubai half the year and sipping on whisky as I discussed politics. But I could have chosen to show up as a dad. I could have been there for Lily and Dan in any way I knew how. I could have chosen to value people above my ego. I could have chosen my family over the booze. I could have changed when I promised I would. All of those little moments that I let pass me by every day, those were all the paths I could have taken. And yet, here I was. Sat on the pavement all alone, smoking fags and lying to my only daughter. Here I was, still, after all of this time, choosing not to change. I could have stayed at home that night instead of travelling to Pembrokeshire. Why the fuck did I have to choose that path? I so desperately didn't want the pictures in my head, replaying over and over again of my precious girl in the woods that night. I didn't want to see it anymore.

Three cigarettes and an empty can later, I made my way through the back gate and into the garden. It was just me on the job today and the couple inside hadn't seemed to notice I'd taken a break, or at least, they didn't feel the need to hound me for it which I was grateful for. My rake was still balanced against the wall and it was as if the last half an hour of my life hadn't even happened. I picked up the rake and started back to work, clinging onto the sound of Lily's sweet voice. Even when she was angry, she still sounded like my little girl. I pictured the seven-year-old I had left behind that night all those years ago. I willed her to still be that seven-year-old with the world at her feet.

Danny

It was 6am when they loudly bashed on the door. We had all been fast asleep, peacefully ignorant to the way in which our world was about to be shattered. I was the first to the door. I could feel the energy shift as I reached to open it. I knew it was now time. We got to the police station and they walked me immediately to the interview room. They weren't fucking around this time.

"This interview is being tape recorded and may be given in evidence if your case is brought to trial. We are in interview room 2 at Haverfordwest police station. The date is the 3rd March and the time by my watch is 6:42am. I am Detective Constable Jenkins. The other police officer present is Detective Constable Dent. Please state your full name and date of birth"

"Daniel Draker. 17th February 2006"

"Do you agree that there are no other persons present?"

"Yes"

136

"Before the start of this interview, I must remind you that you are entitled to free and independent legal advice either in person or by telephone at any stage. Do you wish to speak to a legal advisor now or have one present in the interview?"

"No"

"Right Daniel, we all know why we are here so you can all save us a lot of time if you just fess up now"

"I don't know what you're talking about", I responded.

"On the night of the 17th February 2024, you murdered Ayla Stevens".

"No, I didn't"

"For the record, I am now showing Daniel Draker a photo of evidence piece 15 and 16". He placed the photos down in front of me and looked me dead in the eye. A look that promised me that this time I was trapped. I didn't speak.

"This is your shirt isn't it, Daniel?" He didn't wait for me to answer, "This is your shirt covered in Ayla Stevens blood. And wrapped inside your shirt is the knife you stabbed her with, covered in her blood and swarming with your fingerprints". I felt it then. My heart drop to my stomach, my world flip upside down. This was it. There was no going back from here. They had found actual evidence. They had the murder weapon.

"I am going to ask you again Daniel. You murdered Ayla Stevens, didn't you?" I took a big gulp of water before staring him directly in the eye, determined to keep face,

"No comment".

My mind started to whir then. I didn't think they had found the knife. I wasn't sure how thorough I had been at covering the tracks of that evening but it was clear that all the stones had finally been turned over and they had discovered where I had hidden it on that stormy Saturday night. They now had a clear motive and the murder weapon. I could almost hear them locking the door and throwing away the key.

I walked out of the interview room with the detectives on either side of me. They lobbied me over to the desk where a small man was sat behind a protective screen.

"Daniel Draker, on the 5th March 2024, you are being charged with first degree murder with intent. You are not eligible for parole and you will remain here until your trial begins". I didn't flinch as he read it out. The only thing running through my head was how many people had tried spitting at that man over the years he had worked here. It can't be an easy job. I felt a bizarre feeling of sympathy swaddle me. The tension in the officers' shoulders beside me relaxed and my attention shifted to how they were feeling. I guess this was a triumph for them. Perhaps if I spent enough time thinking about how everyone else was doing, I wouldn't have to acknowledge myself.

The officers led me down the corridor and guided me into a cell where I was told I would have to wait until they could transfer me. They didn't indicate how long that may be; for how long would I have to call these four walls my home? The door clanged shut and there was an eerie silence that chimed a long, never-ending tune. I was alone. I did everything I could to avoid thinking about the gravity of the situation I was in. My god, I was not ready to believe that this could be my life. I cradled myself into a ball and sat next to the left wall, clutching my knees up to my chest. This isn't happening. This isn't happening, I prayed over and over. But it was.

Part 2
The trial

One year, two months and fourteen days later

Day One: opening statements

Daniel lay on the cold hard bed and stared up at the grey, peeling ceiling of his cell. The world sat silently. Over the last year, he had become accustomed to the silence before dusk. It was his favourite time of the day. He inhaled deeply and listened as the air entered through his nose and whistled back out pass his lips. He pictured his lungs shriveling up like a balloon as the air escaped from him. Every morning, he lay perfectly still, imagining if Ayla's last breaths felt as peaceful as his were now. He had been surprised by quite how quickly he had become accustomed to his new life. The simplicity of his new normal offered a calm which he hadn't foreseen. All of the things he thought had mattered on the outside just didn't seem so important in here.

The serenity was eventually broken by the clanging of the prison doors and yells from men who didn't used to be the shade of anger they are now. It was a rage that had been so carefully moulded from every locked door and shaking of the head. They had each been painted different shades of red over years of torment; with each stroke adding to a masterpiece of wrath. It was a fury so certain that it was deemed to be part of the normal here. Daniel pulled himself out of bed and slowly got dressed. Daniel did everything slowly here since there was nothing but time to waste. *Better to waste away time than to waste away sanity,* an inmate had told him on his second day inside when Daniel had questioned why he was counting the number of spoons used during the lunch hour. Daniel laughed at the irony, certain that guy had already long lost his mind. That was, until the very next day when a massive bloke had lamped a member of the kitchen staff because there weren't any spoons to eat his dessert with. *128 spoons. He should have known there were only 128 spoons,* the inmate leaned over and whispered to Daniel. Daniel had smiled and whispered back: *insanity prevails.*

Daniel hadn't made friends inside. He had been careful not to. He had believed that making friends would be resigning himself to the idea that he was here for the long haul. He hadn't thought it was worth forming attachments with people who he believed were fundamentally different from him. All of the men in here were guilty. He was not.

The prison officer came and knocked on Daniel's door and guided him into a holding cell where he was asked to stand at the edge of the room, alongside three other inmates. The guards ordered them to take off their clothes and put their arms up ready to be searched. Daniel had only experienced the strip search once before when he was first placed in prison over a year ago where he was to wait for the court date. His cheeks flushed red as the guard inspected every inch of his body. The other three inmates looked a lot older than him and as if this humiliation was normal for them. Daniel however, felt a deep sense of shame swathe him as he asked to lift up his penis and testicles for the man to get a closer look. He prayed for it to be over as he stared up towards the ceiling.

Once the strip search was finally complete, Daniel was handed the suit he had chosen for court. As he did up the jacket, he felt a sense of humanity return to his bones. He was no longer a number but a person again. It felt so good to have something which fit him after all of this time. He hadn't wanted to wear a suit at first. He had never worn one before and he thought it made him look like a bit of a tosser. But Paul, his appointed lawyer, had insisted. He had said it would make him look like he was taking the case seriously. He had told Daniel that showing up in jeans looks sloppy.

"Looks matter mate, particularly to a jury", he had said. Daniel had so desperately wanted to refute him but he knew he was right. Because people don't want to believe that murderers wear suits.

The guards handcuffed and shackled him before walking out to the car which was parked just behind the door but on the near side of the gates. The fresh air smacked Daniel across the face. It was mid-June and the birds were chirping their summer tune. Daniel had never thought he would care about birds singing before but he couldn't help but smile as he listened. He felt like he had aged twenty years already. He was strapped into the bus

142

and leaned his head on the seat in front of him, feeling waves of motion sickness overwhelm him. It had been a long time since he had been in a moving vehicle and he felt claustrophobia melt into him; he mused at how it had not once taken hold of him in the cell. As the bus rode over the bumps, the weight of the restraints began to dig into his ankles. The journey only lasted eighteen minutes but Daniel was relieved when the van finally pulled up outside the courthouse. The opening doors were a welcome relief.

The cameras gathered outside the court house and the journalists bustled past each other, all frantically trying to get as close to the steps as possible. No one dared cross that bottom step or they wouldn't be allowed back the following day. There were stringent rules about photography inside the courthouse itself for which Daniel was relieved. The idea of his body language and expressions being picked apart by journalists in such a heightened and stressful situation was almost as unbearable as the trial itself. Daniel had never been a fan of cameras even before now. He always thought photographs were only for one of two things: vanity or criticism. And he wasn't feeling particularly narcissistic.

The van pulled up at 8:53am and Daniel was escorted inside, shielded by the guards from the flashing cameras and microphones being forced in his direction. He was surprised to feel a flash of self-importance blaze through his veins after all. Even still, he held his head low and his hands were by his belly shackles, palms together with handcuffs around his wrists. He had been given over a year to prepare for this moment. His head spun with thoughts of how things could have been different. He knew that regardless of the outcome of this trial, his life would never be the same again. Trial by media has a 100% hit rate of finding people guilty after all.

As he walked into the court room and took his seat next to his lawyers, he caught eyes with Lily. She was sat in the second row. She wore black jeans and a baby blue turtle neck jumper. Her hair was in a loose pony tail and her makeup was understated. She sat with her mum on one side and her dad on the other. Hayley was wearing a floral dress, completely inappropriate for the occasion, and Gavin was wearing a suit not much dissimilar to Daniel's. Daniel didn't make eye contact with either of them.

He pulled out his chair as Paul whispered something into his ear and Daniel nodded. There was no mistaking how young he looked next to the grown-up adults he was surrounded by. It looked as though he was on work experience, playing dress up. Paul had told Daniel to wear the suit because it made him look serious, but he really knew that it made him look young. Paul was desperate for the jury to see Daniel for what he was; a child.

The command for everyone to rise bellowed out from the speakers and the whole court room took to their feet as the judge walked in with a purpose and confidence that could only be acquired from twenty years of experience. Daniel looked over to the jury. Twelve men and woman who would decide his fate. They all looked so scared, so unsure of themselves in a way that filled Daniel with unease. He desperately wanted to go over to them, to introduce himself and explain the terrible mistake that had happened. He wanted just five minutes to say his truthful piece.

But instead, he sat facing forward in his chair whilst they scrutinized his every move.

The judge rose to his feet and read out the charges against Daniel, asking him to clearly state his plea for the court room. "Not guilty" he responded with conviction. The judge then laid out the procedures, stating that the trial was expected to last between three to five days. Daniel sat with his eyes fixated on the ground. The court room didn't smell like his cell and he was starting to feel nauseous from the overstimulation of his senses. He had been desperately anticipating this moment for months and now that it was finally here, he wanted nothing more than to be back in the safety of his four walls, staring at the ceiling and counting the specks of dust that he could see.

The prosecutor took to the floor. He was a thirty-four-year-old man with sparkling blue eyes and a captivating voice. He introduced himself as John Seines. He stood tall and paced around the room, going back and forth from the jury, looking each member in the eye as he laid out his opening statement.

On the 17th February 2024, Ayla Stevens was brutally murdered in Boddington Park in North West Wales. She had been enjoying a night out with her girlfriend when she was savagely attacked by Mr Daniel Draker outside of the pub. All Ayla wanted that night was to get back home to her loving parents. However, Mr. Daniel Draker had other plans. What I will prove to you over the next few days is the undeniable truth that Daniel Draker murdered Ayla Stevens that night. Not only this, but he did so with a malice, *cruelty and premeditation which can only be met with the fiercest of sentences. Daniel Draker is a manipulative, callous and cold-blooded killer. Ayla's parents will never get to hold their daughter again, nothing will bring her back. The very least we can give them is the justice that they deserve, the justice that Ayla deserves.*

It was powerful the way he spoke. His words ebbed and flowed as if he had been singing. He spoke with such conviction, almost as if he had been a witness to the murder himself. A few of the jurors bowed their heads towards the floor, the weight of the trial sinking in. Over the next few days, they would endure listening to the story which led to a teenager being wiped from this world as if she had no right to be in it. In just a few days, they would have to find Daniel either guilty or innocent of a crime so heinous that for most it was incomprehensible. They needed to be sure of their verdict; not merely because it was their duty but because it would weigh on their own conscious. It would plait its way into the fiber of who they became from here on out.

Daniel turned his head back toward Lily, sandwiched in between their two parents. Her head was bowed but her eyes looked forward, a steady glare burning through him. He couldn't tell if it was a glare of sympathy or anger and he didn't know which would be worse. He desperately wanted to hug her. He yearned to feel her heart, a beating reassurance that life would go on after all of this was over. Maybe if he hugged her, his own heart could go with hers and explore the world and feel all of the things he might not ever get the chance to. The gravity of the situation set on Daniel as John Seines took his seat back down at the table. Daniel had coped with the last year in prison because he had known this day would come. He had been ticking off the dates in his diary since he was put behind bars. The idea of ticking off another twenty-odd years' worth of dates made his blood run cold.

He felt Paul tugging at the sleeves of his shirt, fiddling with his cufflink as his leg shook up and down. Daniel hadn't been able to afford an experienced lawyer so this was only Paul's second case of his career. He had won his first case 'against all odds' as he so generously put it. He wasn't young. He had a mid-life crisis in his forties and had re-trained as a barrister. He had been in some dead-end marketing job for seventeen years and in his words had *climbed the ladder and realised the view was fucking dull.* Daniel realised during the re-telling of that story that this was merely a job for Paul, 'an exciting view'; he couldn't bear the thought that his life behind bars might just be Paul's learning curve.

The energy shifted in the room as eyes turned towards their table. It was Paul's moment now. First impressions count. He pushed his chair out from next to Daniel, brushed down his suit, took a deep breath and waltzed onto the floor. He gave off an air of loud confidence which Daniel so desperately wanted to believe in. He sat up in his seat and said a silent prayer in his head as Paul's words bellowed throughout the room.

Ladies and gentleman of the jury. My client, Daniel Draker, is innocent of this crime of which he is being accused. I implore you

147

to consider the facts of this case throughout the trial and not be guided by trifling heresy or emotions. Daniel was indeed, a young boy who was struggling to come to terms with his sister's sexuality. However, let me be crystal clear; this struggle is not indicative of murder. This struggle is not a motive as the prosecution would like you to believe. Through looking at the facts of the case, I am confident you will find that my client did not murder Ayla Stevens. It would be a tragedy to allow for a young, innocent boy to lose his life over a crime he did not commit. His fate is in your hands and we must get this right.

The hushed murmurs among the gallery were telling. It felt as if round one had already been lost and it would be a long climb back up to the top. Paul had made the fatal mistake of drawing attention to the motive. It didn't matter that he was disagreeing with it; it was now the front and center of everyone's mind. Daniel had a motive, and a strong one at that. John Seines sat smugly, jotting down a few notes with a ballpoint black pen and looking as if the world owed him something. Daniel himself, looked as though he was being swallowed up. His body was reclining into itself as he made himself smaller in his chair, his suit suddenly looking like it swamped his body. Only a few rows back, Gavin sat with that same resigned posture, the two mirroring one another. He was all too familiar with how this process went.

The gallery quietened back down and the judge stood up, outlining the process for the next few days to come. He explained that court would begin at 9am sharp every morning and would break for lunch at 12:30pm for one hour exactly. He was clear with the jury that they should not discuss any details of the case outside of the court house or they would risk being removed from the case. They were not allowed to research the case at all, nor Daniel or Ayla. Daniel couldn't help but wonder what they would find if they did. He had remembered seeing a few articles after he had been charged. Some of the inmates had purposefully left on the news channel or shoved papers in his face when they were eating lunch; all part of the hazing process it seemed. They had all been click-bait heaven.

Teenage boy murders sister's secret lover.

Murder: the price of love.

Bigot murders lesbian lover.

Each one had seemed to become more and more entrenched in a guilt that was still yet to be decided. Trial by media had already decided his sentence over a year ago.

After the judge had explained the landscape of the next few days, he adjourned court for the day. Daniel couldn't believe how short the time in the courtroom had been. He was escorted back into a waiting room with the other inmates and was given a brown paper bag with a ham and cheese sandwich, an apple and a bottle of water inside. He sat there, silently chewing down his lunch, feeling like he was on the strangest school trip in the world.

The public scurried out of the room and piled out into the corridors. Lily stood next to her mum and dad, waiting for everyone else to filter out back onto the streets. She was keen to avoid the reporters for as long as possible but she knew it was an inevitability she would have to face at some point.

As Lily glanced down the corridor towards the front doors of the courthouse, she caught eyes with Ayla's dad. The lightning bolts of fear radiated through her as they had done the day of Ayla's funeral. But this time round, his eyes did not soften as they locked eyes with each other. Instead, they narrowed and glazed over with a dark and assuring rage; an anger that did not threaten danger but rather vowed an unwavering guilt. Lily desperately wanted to hold his stare, to tell him her story through the silence. She wanted him to know how she wished none of this had ever happened, how deeply she missed Ayla. But her eyes gave way and flickered from the hypnosis she was trapped in.

After the flurry of chaos had flooded and dissipated onto the streets outside the courthouse, Daniel was escorted by a prison guard on either side of him, back to the van. He was guided into the backseat, his wrists back in handcuffs. As he sat with his hands on his lap and his body slumping into the seat, his eyes darted out of the window. He desperately tried to soak up every moment of the mundaneness of life he could gather. He saw a man listening to his headphones and he wondered what song he might be listening to. He noticed a woman with her child jogging hand in hand into a corner shop and he pondered why they were in such a hurry. How lucky they were to have somewhere to be. For a momentary second, Ayla flashed across his mind. He saw her body lying lifeless on the ground, imagined it being slowly decomposed by the bugs surrounding her. He considered what she might have been doing now if she wasn't dead. But just as quickly as she had flashed into his mind, she was gone. He knew couldn't afford to think of Ayla right now. He couldn't risk the unravelling of feelings that might follow. For the next five days, he had to stay focussed on the task at hand; he had to stay focussed on nothing but his innocence.

Day Two: The prosecution

Gavin woke up as the sun blinded him through the window. He had rented a small one-bedroom flat in Pembrokeshire for the duration of the trial. He had never dreamed that this would be the circumstances under which him and his son would rekindle their relationship, if you could call it that. But Danny had called him up when he was in remand,

"I want you to be there Dad," he had said calmly over the phone. Perhaps it was because Gavin knew what it was like, perhaps Daniel had wanted the reassurance of someone who had been through this hell before and might be able to impart some wisdom on the process. Or perhaps it was because Daniel needed Gavin to bear witness to the destruction he had contributed towards. Perhaps Daniel blamed Gavin for the choices he had made. Whatever the reason, Gavin didn't have to be asked twice. He packed his bag that same day and had left it waiting by the door until the court date was set. He hopped on the train a few days before the trial and picked up the keys for the apartment he had found which was as close to the court house as possible. He had settled into bed the night before with a wave of excitement crashing over him. He knew he shouldn't be feeling excited. He knew it was wrong to bask in his son's terror but he let the thrill fester for a little while longer before batting it away. It had been ten years since he had seen his son after all and the anticipation fizzed inside of him.

Lily and Hayley too woke up early. After the opening statements yesterday, they had got a taxi home, ordered a takeaway and sat in silence together watching a quiz show of which neither of them knew any of the answers. Hayley had been sober for just over four months now, truly and genuinely sober, and not just the kind of sobriety she used to claim. She had joined a support network not long after Danny had been charged. It had taken her the first few months to actually engage in a way which would make a difference, but to everyone's amazement (not in the least Hayley's herself), she actually started getting better. She would have almost certainly quit in those first few months if it hadn't been for Lily.

Lily had become a different person entirely since Danny had been charged. Hayley had never seen someone so broken. It hadn't been the stereotypical brokenness either. It was almost a silent manifestation. She had been a witness to the shattering of Lily's entire being. She had been a helpless bystander as she watched her only daughter wither away in front of her own eyes. She watched as a hollow vacancy poisoned her soul. And as she watched, she felt a deep and unending guilt smother her. It dawned on her then that she couldn't save Lily from drowning when she could barely even stay afloat herself. First, she would need to learn how to swim.

She had a few slips in the first few weeks and months of course. A drug affair doesn't disappear overnight but it seemed that she was getting stronger with every day that passed. She felt a sense of pride she had never felt before. It was magnetic. It was addictive. She couldn't help but wonder if she had managed all of this a few years back whether Danny would not be where he is. She decided not to dwell on that nagging question for too long at any one time for she was certain she sadly already knew the answer.

Lily woke up to the sound of her alarm and rolled across the bed, fumbling for her phone to turn off the piercing ringing. She was missing school over the next few days while the trial was happening. Her teachers hadn't really known what to say to her on Friday as she left at the end of the day. Mr Potts had earnestly said that he hoped *next week goes well.* As Lily had walked back home that afternoon, she considered what *well* would look like but wasn't sure if she would be able to recognise it given the circumstances. Still, it had been better than Miss Jameson's wish of *good luck.* Lily had laughed, knowing that luck had nothing to do with it. She was sure that whatever would happen at this trial had been carefully curated by Danny. It would not be luck which found him guilty or innocent; it would be meticulous planning on his part, for that, she was sure. She pulled back the covers of her duvet and swung her legs round, sitting on the edge of the bed for a couple of minutes before mustering the strength to actually stand up.

Hayley and Lily sat in silence again, eating their breakfast and drinking their coffee, too frightened of the words they might say. They spent more time together now that Hayley was sober but conversation was still somehow stunted. It is hard to find the words after ten years of learning to disappear from one another in every which way. Hayley's support group had suggested that family counselling would be a good step forward to try and mend those broken relationships. But when Hayley had brought it up to Lily, she had said it wouldn't be right to do family counselling when they weren't a family, not without Dan.

Today was the prosecution and if the opening statements had been anything to go by yesterday, they both knew that they could be in for an absolute car crash. They weren't ready to prepare for a life if this didn't go the way they hoped. This sentence was not just for Dan, but for Hayley and Lily too. Lily braced herself for the scours she would get from Ayla's parents and grandparents as she walked through the courtroom doors. Yesterday had been bad enough and she feared their glares burning into her, screaming at how none of this would have happened if it wasn't for her, a constant reminder that this was all her fault.

When they had finally finished their breakfast, they called an uber and waited outside the front door for it to arrive. The silver Toyota pulled up after four minutes and the driver had the radio playing as they opened the door to the backseat. Lily was grateful

154

for the mindless chatter of the radio hosts as she stared out the back window. She did everything she could not to think about Ayla but there were ghosts of her lifeless and decaying body haunting every street they drove past. She had spent weeks and months trying to forget Ayla completely; erase her from her memory as if she never even existed. But Ayla always echoed in the silences of Lily's life, devastating any chance of peace. They say that grief is the price of loving but if that was true, Lily made a vow to never love again, for nothing was worth this raw and never-ending cycle of pain.

"Have a great day", chirped the taxi man before they slammed the doors behind them. The heat from the sun pounded the back of Lily's head as she walked up the steps to the courthouse. It wasn't even 9am but the heat was palpable. She had used to love summer but she felt the appreciation of these sunny days dissipate as she knew how the warmth beating down on her would forever remind her of these moments; waiting outside a courthouse for her brother to likely be convicted of a crime she wished had never happened in the first place. The feel of the sun would now only ever shine a light on what could have been and the roads not taken.

Daniel woke up early again. He had been so exhausted when he had got in yesterday that he had passed out almost immediately. He hadn't realised the toll that the case would take. It was a combination of the adrenaline and the nerves which was draining in the most toxic way. It was a type of tiredness that didn't feel earnt.

He waited patiently for the door to be unlocked and to be escorted from the four walls he had called home for the last year. Today he felt more prepared for the strip search than yesterday and the colour on his face was less evident than it had been previously. He still felt that same sense of humiliation wash over him as he stood naked in the small, stuffy and hot room. After it was finished, he was piled into the van and sat in the back with a prison guard next to him, his hands cuffed together and resting delicately in his lap.

He imagined Paul waking up and having a shower, putting on his smart suit and fancy aftershave. He imagined him walking down the stairs of his fancy house and kissing his wife and kids' goodbye. He pictured him driving in his fancy car listening to some bullshit podcast about how success is a choice and discipline is the tool to the top.

Today was prosecution day. Paul had already made very clear to Daniel that today would be intense, that it may feel like they are losing, that the scales would look to be tipping only one way. But he had also assured him that they would get their moment, they would have the chance to respond, to rebalance the scales. Daniel only had to trust him.

The court room was packed out. It felt even busier than the day before. All of the reporting benches were filled and the gallery was brimming with Ayla's family and friends, sat next to random strangers who had taken an interest in the case. The strangers sat relaxed, back in their chairs and excitedly anticipated the gory details, the minutia and specifics of the case. They would shake their heads in disbelief and may even shed a tear at a particularly poignant moment. Because for them, this was purely a spectacle, something to be fascinated by. It was as if they were merely watching a television programme. They had no skin in the game. They wouldn't feel the anguish that Daniel felt, nor the pressure that Paul held. They wouldn't feel the fear that sat deep in Hayley or the guilt that knotted in Lily's stomach. They wouldn't feel the weight that the jurors carried nor the heartbreak of Ayla's parents. They wouldn't have to feel any of it, instead observing just above the surface, through a lens of fiction and fantasy.

Everyone rose as the judge entered the room and then settled quickly back into their seats. Daniel glanced at the time. 9:02am. Ayla's parents sat in the front row, their hands entwined in one another's, thinking that maybe they wouldn't break in two if they just held each other tightly enough. This was all they had now. The promise of justice. The concept had made them wince. *I hope you get justice*, people had said, as they shook their hands or held them in an uncomfortable hug at the funeral of their only daughter. They said it in a way that somehow justice might make everything better again, like it would mean they could continue on with their lives, and smile and breathe comfortable breaths. But they both knew that justice wouldn't fix the aching sorrow wedged so deeply inside. They knew justice wouldn't comfort them as they woke screaming from the terrors in the night. They knew justice wouldn't be able to mend their shattered hearts. Justice wouldn't bring back their baby girl.

"All rise". Everyone took to their feet as the judge purposefully marched into the courtroom. The energy shifted as she did.

"Be seated", she bellowed out to the sea of people in the gallery. Everyone quickly shuffled back into their seats, as if they had come in late to the cinema. The first witness was called to the stand. Detective Inspector Jenkins. Daniel's skin crawled as he walked up past him towards the stand. He hadn't seen him since the day he had been arrested and he had found himself fantasizing about being back in the interview room again. He had imagined all the things he might have said in another universe, all of the secrets he might have shared. He lay in bed at night picturing Jenkins face as he told him about the way his father had hurt him. He wondered whether he would have hugged him as tears rolled down his face. He imagined telling him about the truth about what had happened that February night but every time he did, he saw a blank face staring back. Perhaps there was never a universe with a different ending after all.

"I do solemnly, sincerely and truly declare and affirm that the evidence I shall give shall be the truth the whole truth and nothing but the truth", he announced purposefully to the jury in front of her. This was his least favourite part of the job.

"Please introduce yourself to the jury", John nodded at him.

"I am Detective Inspector Jenkins and I was the officer in charge of the investigation".

"Thank you, Detective Inspector Jenkins".

"What was it that first led you to suspect Mr Daniel Draker as a possible suspect in this case?"

"He was a suspect pretty much from the get-go. We requested that he come in for a significant witness interview but he refused. We shortly gained enough evidence to warrant an arrest"

"I see. So, Daniel originally refused to be interviewed in this case?"

"That's correct, yes".

"And what was the evidence that you gained which led to his first arrest?"

"We gained CCTV evidence from outside of the pub". The sides of John's mouth raised ever so slightly.

"We are going to play this CCTV evidence for the jury now, thank you". The jurors' eyes flickered across the room to the big screen. Daniel watched too. He watched as Ayla appeared in the frame of the video. He watched as he moved towards her as she taunted him. He watched as his hand curled into a fist and swung across the cold night air, colliding with the center of her face. He watched as blood poured from her nose and he watched as he turned his body and walked away as if nothing had happened at all. When the video stopped playing, he glanced his eyes over towards Ayla's parents sitting in the front row. This was the last time they would ever see their daughter alive; this is the memory that would sear into the back of their minds as they tried to sleep at night. Her mother was sat, rigid, her steely-eyed gaze staring at the screen. She wished more than anything that she was there that night to protect her daughter so instead, she would be here now. She would not shy away from the horror but instead hold her daughter tightly with her eyes through the screen. *I'm here now Ayla, mummy's here.*

"What did Mr Daniel Draker have to say about this CCTV evidence when he was questioned?"

"He said he had got angry but that he didn't kill her".

"Was he arrested after this interview?"

"No, he was not. CPS said the evidence was too circumstantial to warrant a charge at that stage".

"What happened next in your investigation?"

"We had a witness come forward with the murder weapon and bloodied t-shirt. We were able to conduct analysis on these items and discovered both Daniel Draker's fingerprints and DNA. We then arrested him for a second time and he was charged with the murder of Ayla Stevens".

"Thank you, Detective Inspector Jenkins, that will be all". John smiled and walked back over towards his seat. The judge then called up Paul for his first cross-examination. There was an uncertainty settling in the air and Daniel was sure it wasn't just him who could feel it.

"Detective Inspector Jenkins, I am Paul Grange. I would like to ask you about your earlier comment", he paused, "when you said that Mr Daniel Draker was a suspect 'pretty much from the get-go', what did you mean by this?"

"Mr Daniel Draker was a significant witness in this case and he refused to be interviewed early on in our investigation. That raised suspicions for me and I am sure you can see why".

"I'm afraid I can't see why Detective. My understanding is that a voluntary interview is just that: voluntary. My client was therefore under no obligation to attend this".

"Of course. It is his right to decline the interview but that does not mean that suspicions were not raised because of this. Most witnesses are eager to give the police as much information as possible". Paul started to walk up and down the floor now.

"How many cases have you been the leading officer for Detective Inspector Jenkins?"

"Forty-two including this one"

"And in those other cases, have the witnesses always react how you 'expect' them to?"

"I don't ever expect a witness to react in any which way. Everyone is different"

"Ah!" Paul exclaimed, "But it would seem that you *did* expect my client to behave in a certain way. You expected him to give a voluntary interview. And when he did not react or behave in the way you expected, you presumed that this was an assumption of his guilt".

"That is incorrect", Jenkins retorted, very matter-of-factly.

"And then assuming his guilt, you searched for evidence which would confirm these suspicions, isn't that right?"

"That is incorrect".

"It is clear to me that this investigation was flawed from the very start. My client was assumed to be guilty simply for executing his legal right. This investigation has been prejudiced, with investigators only pursuing lines of enquiry which reflected this flawed rhetoric. Your investigation created an echo chamber of guilt, is that not correct Detective?"

"That is incorrect", he repeated.

"That will be all, no more questions". Jenkins stood down from the stand and walked confidently back through the gallery. He had been in enough cases to know how it worked. The first time she had been accused of bias, it had shaken him. He had gone home and poured a large glass of whisky and sat in silence on the sofa as his words fears bounced around in his head; that a guilty man might walk free. But soon he realised that this was almost protocol in a case like this one, it was all part of the play.

Daniel glanced around in the silence between the witnesses. The room seemed so dark compared to the brightness of the outside. The judge called the second witness up to the stand and Daniel held his breath. When he had been given a list of witnesses a few weeks back, this was the one that cut him the deepest.

He walked up to the stand with his head towards the ground, his shoulders hunched. Daniel would have recognised that stature anywhere. It was Ben. He held up his right hand.

"I do solemnly, sincerely and truly declare and affirm that the evidence I shall give shall be the truth the whole truth and nothing but the truth" He didn't dare look Daniel in the eye as much as Daniel willed him to. Ben had toyed for weeks over his duty to share his account with the police. He had endured sleepless nights questioning as to what was more important; his loyalty as a friend or his duty to share the truth. Daniel should have known that Ben was bound to speak out eventually. He had always been a good man, even when he was still just a boy. It was one of the reasons why they had become such good friends in the first place; Daniel had been magnetically drawn to the moral compass which Ben possessed.

The prosecutor painstakingly asked Ben to talk through the details of February 17th, down to the jokes that had been made and the drinks that had been brought. Daniel sat and watched Ben as he spoke, transfixed by his account of that evening. He was surprised by how many of the details he seemed to remember and as he listened, the shadow of the night rested its hand on his shoulder. It was a steady weight, reminding Daniel that the memory of what had happened would always be there, reminding him that the regret he felt would linger long beyond this case alone.

Ben continued on, explaining how he had left the pub once it had shut but that Daniel had been gagging for a night 'out out'. He stated that he hadn't seen Ayla leave the pub but that he was unlikely to know if she had. As he put it, Ayla and he weren't friends and he barely knew her.

"In your opinion Ben, what were Daniel's feelings towards Ayla Stevens?"

"He didn't like her".

"Can you expand on that please? Why didn't Daniel like Ayla?"

"Well, he never exactly said it, but I reckon he knew about Lils and her and-"

"I'm sorry, could you please state who this 'Lils' person you are referring to is for the sake of the jury" he interrupted.

"Oh yeah, my bad. Lily is Danny's sister. We never spoke about it but I reckon he knew that Ayla and Lily were a couple and he wouldn't have liked that, that's for sure".

Lily shrunk into her seat, wishing the moment to be over. She had known that her and Ayla's relationship was bound to be a focus of the trial but she could feel her skin crawl whenever her name was mentioned. She felt some of the eyes from the jury land on her and it felt like they were studying her outside in. The prosecutor let out a small ceremonial laugh,

"Didn't like her," he walked over to the jury. "Let us take a look now at a text thread between Daniel and Ben in the days leading up to Ayla's murder. I will leave it up to the jury if what you read is mere 'dislike' as Ben has put it".

Daniel: I'm so fucking fed up with that bitch
Ben: Who?
Daniel: Ayla fucking Stevens. She wouldn't deal me. Gurl's a class A twat mate. I can't wait till some1 gives it 2 her.
Ben: Mate don't worry about it. I'll get Baz to sort us out. No dramas.
Daniel: She needs some1 to put her ten feet under u get me.

The silence was deafening. Ben took a sip of water from his glass and fiddled with the wrist of his jumper. The prosecutor pushed on,

"Can you explain to the jury what this conversation was in relation to?" Ben took a deep breath, feeling suddenly acutely aware of the accusatory glares pressing his way. For some, Ben would seem complicit in what had happened. For Ben himself, the guilt of what had happened would surely eat away at him for the rest of his life, the what-ifs he would contemplate as he tossed and turned at night. Daniel was sure Ben would always now hold their friendships in his file of regrets and he felt a deep sadness in thinking the memories which they shared together were now tainted in a bad light.

"We had wanted to get some cocaine for a party we were going to and Ayla had refused to deal to Dan. It had annoyed him".

"As far as you are aware, did Ayla ever deal drugs to Daniel?"

"Maybe a couple times I guess." He paused. "But she liked toying with him. Ayla loved winding Dan up. She would often say she would deal him and then not show up just to mess with him. She knew exactly which buttons to push and it's like she couldn't help herself sometimes". There was a silence which rung out across the room; a silence all too familiar in crimes against women and girls. A silence that screamed: *did she deserve it? Was this actually all her fault after all?*

John continued, seemingly ignoring what had just been said.

"In the days after Ayla's murder, how did Daniel present to you Ben?"

"Umm, I dunno. He was quiet. He didn't want to talk about what had happened". Daniel glanced down towards the table,

165

wondering how he could have acted to make it ok. He wondered what type of reaction would quell the jurors' wandering minds. What would the right reaction have been to a murder in their eyes? "Did this seem strange to you?" Ben glanced over to Dan whose eyes now lay firmly staring at the ground.

"Umm, I guess a little. Just because it was all everyone was talking about". John paused, weighing up how much further he wanted to go.

"In your opinion Ben, do you believe that Daniel could have murdered Ayla?" A pause. It was as if everyone was holding their breath in that silence. The slightest nod of his head,

"I do, yeah". John twirled round as if on stage. Ben bowed his head and glanced back over towards Daniel. Their eyes locked for half-a-second before Ben looked away again. He felt guilt and relief and shame twist in his stomach, pulling a knot so tight that it was bound to forever exist deep inside of him.

The courtroom continued to buzz with the sound of hushed chatter and reverberating shock bouncing off the walls. Ben had been Daniel's friend after all. He, of all people, surely ought to believe in Daniel's innocence. The judge shushed the murmurs in the gallery and gave the power of the silence back to John.

"Thank you, Ben, no further questions". John took his time making his way back towards his seat, sure to let the aftershocks last as long as possible. Daniel stared at each of the jurors in turn and saw their heavy, sunken eyes staring back. They already looked weathered, he thought. One of the women had been excited when she had received the letter through her door that Thursday afternoon.

"Jury duty!" she had screamed down the phone to her parents. "I got jury duty! I hope it's something interesting like a murder or something like that". Her wishes now rung in her ears like nails screeching down a blackboard. She didn't want this.

Daniel hated how he could feel the smugness of John and his team reverberate around the gallery. Their confidence melted into the scent of the air and floated across the room, gently gliding past each and every person like some sort of twisted lap of honor. Paul shuffled the paperwork in front of him before taking to the floor. He made his way to his feet and stood proudly in front of the jury box. This was the reason he had wanted to become a solicitor in the first place, this feeling of importance which cloaked him as twelve pairs of eyes stared into him, intently listening to every word he spoke.

"Mr Hill, you say that yourself and Mr Draker were friends, is that correct?"

"That's correct", Ben leaned into the microphone, his voice already sounding like it might close up at any given moment.

"And you were at the pub with Daniel the night of Ayla's death, is that correct?"

"Yes"

"Did you notice anything about Daniel that night that seemed unusual to you?"

"No, not really"

"Did he seem angry that Ayla had come to the pub that night?"

"No"

"Did he say anything to you about the fact that Ayla was there?"

"No, he just generally seemed pretty happy that night"

"I see", Paul paused, "so what is it exactly that made you think that Daniel could be guilty of this crime then?" Ben took a deep breath in.

"I didn't at first. But it was just a combination of little things, I guess. Like I thought he was acting weird in the days after it had happened and then I heard about the punch. And then I just kept reading back old messages between us and I got this bad feeling in my stomach you know. I knew I had to speak to the police then".

"Ah yes, of course!" Paul exclaimed, "the text messages" he paused. "The text messages where Daniel Draker makes a joke about wanting Ayla gone".

"When Daniel sent you that text message Ben, did you think he was being serious about 'burying' Ayla?" The text messages were now blown back up on the screen for the courthouse to analyse again. Incredulity once again rippled throughout the gallery.

"Not at the time no but then what with everything that had happened, I thought it might be relevant". The nerves had dissipated now and Ben was holding himself tall, proud.

"In your testimony Ben, you said that you believe Daniel Draker was capable of killing Ayla Stevens, is that correct?"

"Yes, that's correct", Ben responded.

"Is it the existence of texts such as these that led you to this conclusion?" Ben nodded,

"Partly yeah". Paul pushed on,

"So, you admit that these texts are part of the reason you believe Daniel could have killed Ayla?"

"Yes."

Paul flicked the remote at the screen then and more text messages flashed across the gallery on the big screen.

Ben: Mate, I'm actually gonna kill that girl one day

Daniel: Ayla?

Ben: Yeah, she does my nut in. School would be a hell of a lot better without her there.

Ben: Might suddenly become interested in clay pigeon shooting and get me a shot gun lol

Ben shuffled behind the stand, pushing his weight from one foot onto the other.

"So…" Paul begun, "you believe that text messages are reason enough to suspect someone of murder. If this is the case, then it would seem you too, ought to be on trial Mr Hill".

"Objection" John rose to his feet.

"I am merely highlighting the fact that these text messages do not bear any weight on the facts in this case", Paul politely argued to the judge.

"Sustained" The judge bellowed.

"Was Daniel ever violent towards women or girls Ben? In all of the years that you two have been friends? Have you ever known him to act in a violent way towards women?" Ben shook his head.

"There are no previous alterations which make you think Daniel could be guilty of such a heinous crime?"

"No, I guess not". He was shaken now and Paul weighed up the chances in his head.

"I'm going to ask you again Mr Hill. Do you really think your friend, who has no previous history of being violent towards women, could be a murderer?" There was another pause then and Daniel held his breath.

"No, I don't know. I don't know". And there was the golden ticket, a seed of doubt, another stroke on the picture Paul was desperately trying to paint.

"No", repeated Paul. "No further questions thank you". Ben stepped down from the lectern and sculked off out through the back of the room. Daniel wondered what might be going through his head. A potion of confusion and guilt as he tried to reconcile his own truth.

A forensic expert, Dr Elise Diamond was called to the stand next. She too, held up her right hand and swore to tell the whole truth and nothing but the truth. Her promises felt empty to Daniel. This woman was a stranger after all. He did not know what promises meant to her in the first place.

John began pacing up and down the floor again and circled back round to stand confidently in front of the jury, addressing them directly. He explained how the next piece of evidence which they would examine would be the murder weapon: the kitchen knife. John had pieced together a possible motive through the witness of Ben, the intention of murder painted as evidence through the texts. Next was the weapon. He started off by asking Dr Diamond about the reliability and validity of fingerprint testing. She spoke with conviction, a sureness in her voice which was supported by her status in society.

"We can be sure of our result 99.9% of the time. Of course, with anything, mistakes or misreads can be made. But forensics are extremely reliable forms of evidence indeed".

"Dr Diamond, please can you state to the jury which prints were found on the murder weapon when it was discovered?"

She nodded as if she had just been asked a question in an interview which she had already rehearsed the answer to.

"Certainly." The photo of the knife was pulled up on the screen at the front of the courtroom.

"As you can see here in the different colours, we have three separate prints which were lifted from the knife", the prints were splashed across the knife; all melded and moulded into one another.

"And who do these prints belong to Dr Diamond?"

"They are a match with Hayley Draker, Lily Draker and Daniel Draker". There were more hushed murmurs in the gallery and the judge reminded everyone that they ought to be quiet whilst evidence is being given.

"Ladies and gentlemen of the jury, this was the knife which was found to be missing from the Draker household. It was a knife which would have been used for cooking within the household", John turned his head back towards Dr Diamond then. "What is

171

important for us in this case, is considering who was last to touch this knife, the murder weapon which was used to kill Ayla". He paused. "So, Dr Diamond, through looking at the forensic prints, which of the fingerprints were the last to touch this knife?"

The photo of the knife was displayed, magnified on the screen in the courtroom for all to see. The jurors and the judge, along with Daniel and Paul, each had their own device to examine the photo more carefully. As Dr Diamond spoke, annotations and red lines brushed across the photograph to highlight the different prints that were seen when the knife was examined under the UV light. It felt like a fancy PowerPoint presentation.

"You can see hear that these prints are by far the most significant meaning that these are the prints of relevance in this case. The last person to touch this knife was almost definitely Daniel Draker". She emphasized with such confidence.

Daniel hated the way she never called him a murderer. There was a cryptic-ness to the way she spoke which he loathed. It was as if she was the kid who stood behind the bully and egged them on, never brave enough to get personally involved in the fight. It felt like she could safely hide behind the blanket of science, without ever having to utter the truth she was alluding to, 'Daniel Draker killed Ayla Stevens'

One of the jurors looked over to Daniel as all of this was being laid out, in black and white, to the sea of people in the gallery. Daniel meanwhile, stared at the ground, unflinching. A look which could have so easily been perceived as unremorseful, as callous and sociopathic. He was sure the papers would label it as such. But that same reaction could have been seen across most of the faces in the courtroom, had the juror dared to look. It was not a sign of guilt but rather a resignation of the facts that were being presented.

Dr Diamond went on to state that when the knife had been discovered, Ayla Stevens blood had been all over it. Not only that, but the stab wounds matched with the length of the blade. There was no doubt left in anyone's mind that this had been the murder weapon. And there was no doubt in anyone's mind that Daniel Draker had been the last one to handle it. Dr Diamond was thanked by John and she graciously gave him a wry smile.

There was hardly a break before Paul was up from his seat and pacing up and down the floor of the courthouse. Paul wasn't one for pleasantries.

"Dr Diamond, my name is Paul Grange and I represent Daniel Draker. "For the jury, can you please explain how fingerprint examination works?"

"Certainly" she turned to face the jury, "I start by determining if there is sufficient detail in the fingerprint. In this case, the handle of the knife had plenty of detail in the latent prints. I then take the prints from the handle and compare these details with the prints of a suspect".

"Thank you for that", he smiled before carrying on. "You mentioned in your testimony that there were overlapping prints on the handle of the knife, is that correct?"

"That is correct".

"How are these prints separated from one another?"

173

"Through a process called chemical imaging. We can separate the fingerprints and compare them to different suspects. In this case, the three fingerprints on the handle were Daniel Draker, Lily Draker and Hayley Draker".

"I see. And why did you discard Lily and Hayley's prints?"

"They were not discarded sir. All of the evidence is carefully considered. In this case, through my analysis, it was evident that Daniel Draker was the last person to have contact with the knife". She was becoming agitated now. Dr Diamond had been cross-examined several times. She knew all of the tricks, the ways in which they would try to undermine her.

"I see. So hypothetically speaking Miss Diamond- "

"It's Dr Diamond", she said as she leant in closer to the microphone, looking directly at Paul.

"I am sorry, do forgive me Dr Diamond. Hypothetically speaking, would fingerprints show up on an object which has been handled using gloves?"

"No. Gloves are often used to avoid the detection of finger prints".

"I see," Paul began. "So would it be possible, Dr Diamond, that the suspect used gloves when they handled the murder weapon?"

"Yes, it is possible. But it does beg the question of how said person got hold of the murder weapon which belonged in the Draker household and was found in a spot which only your client knew about". Daniel was taken aback by her sudden willingness to give her own opinions. It seemed Paul felt that same surprise too, and he wondered whether it was in rebuttal to him getting her title wrong.

"But it is important to be clear here Dr Diamond. Someone could have easily used the murder weapon, covering their tracks through using gloves. With this in mind, it makes all the sense in the world for my client's finger prints to be on the handle of the knife considering he would have used this knife regularly in usual cooking procedure in his own home".

"It is indeed possible that someone else could have handled the knife using gloves yes". Daniel flicked his head round to look at his family sitting behind him in the gallery. What was happening felt promising. Paul was stepping up, he thought. Paul addressed the jury then, striding confidently over towards them with a swagger Daniel had not seen before.

"Ladies and gentlemen of the jury. The forensic evidence which has been shared with you is not evidence of a murder. It is evidence of cooking". He smiled as he said it but no one seemed to smile back. Dr Diamond could have even been mistaken to be frowning.

"Thank you, Dr Diamond. I have no further questions". Paul announced. She walked back through the gallery, poised and sure of herself as she had always been.

"The time is now 12:32pm. Court will resume promptly at 1:30pm". The judge announced.

The morning had flown by and Daniel wished for everything to slow down just a little bit. He searched for the air particles across the room, desperately pleading to find some dust in the moment that was passing far too quickly. He wished for the room to look like a memory; a pixelated fade with fraying edges.

It was all happening far too fast and there wasn't enough time to take everything in. He tried to remember everything that had been said; as if he was cramming for an exam that he hadn't revised for. Both he and Paul were escorted into the same room with the dark burgundy sofa and small table where they had debriefed during every lunchtime this week. Paul was sat thoughtfully at the table, eating his sandwich and reading over his notes for the afternoon ahead. Daniel sat opposite him, willing him to give some indicator for how it was going; it felt like it was going well Daniel thought but he couldn't fathom why Paul didn't look pleased. He willed him to smile but instead, he sat with a steely eyed glare, a laser focus on the task ahead.

Ayla's parents were sat just meters away in a separate room, also not speaking. For a trial where there was so much to say, it consistently seemed to stun people into silence. Allison was desperately trying to separate her work from her reality. It was so surreal for her to be in a courthouse and not be on the clock. She couldn't help but think of all of the murder trials she had sat through. In the early days of her career, she had woken in a hot sweat in the middle of the night, shaking at the memories of the testimonies. She had closed her eyes and seen sunken faces and bloody scars and the dark glares of monsters masquerading as men. But as the years ticked by, the testimonies started to lose their shock factor and Allison began to fall asleep at night effortlessly once again. She no longer flinched when she heard of the bruises on the thighs of a dead corpse or how a body had been butchered like a piece of meat. There had been times when she had willed herself to feel the sting of it all. With every case that had passed, she had feared she was slowly losing her humanity. But now, sitting in the box room next to her husband, she drowned in her pain and she began to understand why her brain had protected her for so long. The rest of her life would now be through a lens of unbearable agony. She would go on to fantasise about her own death in a way which had been alien to her before all of this. Time would slowly pass and the rawness of the pain would eventually begin to fade in a way which only promised a lingering guilt would be left behind. A smile would forever be tainted with the knowledge that happiness belonged to everyone else but her. She would never feel peace again.

Everyone begun filing back into the courthouse at 1:20pm. The judge marched back in at 1:25pm and took his seat. He looked refreshed after his lunch break, revitalized in a way that seemed alien to those connected to the case. Daniel and Paul sidled back into their seats and waited with baited breath as the final witness was called to the stand. James. Daniel glanced up as his name was called out and he held up his hand to make his affirmation. Even though he had known James would be testifying against him, he still hadn't truly believed it up until now. James looked smaller than Daniel remembered. The tips of his hair were a peroxide blonde and he was dressed in baggy jeans and an oversized t-shirt. John started off by establishing the relationship, "How do you and Daniel Draker know each other, James?"

"We were at school together. We used to hang out quite a bit, you know, just being dumb kids". He said it like they weren't kids anymore, as if at the ripe old age of nineteen, they suddenly had it all figured out, like there weren't still mistakes to be made, loves to be fumbled, friendships to fizzle.

"And where did you and Daniel tend to hang out?"

"Under the bridge by the park. We used to smoke weed down there". James lacked the consideration that Ben had. He didn't hesitate to mention the weed and Daniel winced at the light it painted him in to the jury. He knew how important the picture they built of him was. It would play such a huge role in if they found him guilty or innocent for this crime. They would be asking themselves, does this boy have it in him to commit such a cold-blooded murder? They would be searching for a sign in his personality that he was capable of it. For some of these people, the knowledge that Daniel did drugs would surely be enough of a reason. Paul had told him before it all started: *the picture we paint of who you are is so much more important than the facts. Juries will only believe the facts which match with their idea of who you are.* Daniel wondered if Paul was sat next to him with the same thoughts running through his brain.

"Tell us a little more about this bridge". The question was vague but James knew what he was searching for so he played along.

"There were a couple loose bricks on one end near the grass. Danny and I used to hide shit, sorry, uh, stuff, there years ago". The prosecutor interrupted, pushing James to be specific,

"What sort of *stuff* did you hide there?"

"We used to put weed and alcohol there, you know, as a sorta hiding place, I guess. And we could just cover it back up with the bricks afterwards". Daniel's face softened slightly, a calm washing over him as he realised where this was headed.

"I see. And did any of your other friends or anyone you know hide anything there? Did you ever find anything that neither of you had placed there?" James shook his head adamantly.

"No. It was only me and Dan. It was like our secret hideout".

"James, please tell the jury what you found behind the bricks on the 1st March 2024?" This time James looked over to Daniel, willing him to make eye contact but Daniel sat like a statue, his eyes burning into the ground.

"There was a knife and a t-shirt with blood stains". Again, mutters fluttered throughout the gallery before being hushed by the judge. "Please take a look at the picture in front of you". A picture of a blood-soaked t-shirt and bloodied knife flashed up on the screen.

"Can you please confirm that these were the items that you discovered that night?" James nodded,

"Yes, that was what I found".

"Thank you, James. That will be all". James darted his eyes across the room, unsure if he was meant to step away.

John turned to face the jury,

"The t-shirt and knife you can see in this picture belong to none other than Daniel Draker. This knife was the one we have just examined which was covered in Ayla's blood and Daniel's fingerprints. And as for the t-shirt. This too, was soaked in Ayla's blood and indeed skin cells were found matching those of exclusively Mr. Daniel Draker". He paused, "Make no mistake. Daniel Draker tried his best to hide the evidence of his crime".

179

John then took a few steps back and took a seat behind his table, giving time for the facts to sink in for the jurors. There was a power in time, there was honesty in the unsaid.

Paul made his way up to the floor as James desperately tried to make eye contact with Daniel from across the room.

"How long have you and Daniel known each other, James?" Paul began.

"Umm, we met in Year 7"

"So quite a long time then. Would you say yourself and Daniel were good friends?"

"Yeah, I'd say so yeah". Daniel looked towards the floor.

"Were you at the pub with Daniel on the night that Ayla was killed?"

"No, I wasn't"

"You weren't out celebrating one of your good friend's 18th birthday? That seems strange. Why weren't you there?" James smiled, the sort of smile every child learns the very first time they are left out of a game they desperately wanted to play.

"I wasn't invited"

"Ah I see, that seems odd considering you were such good friends" he paused, but not long enough for James to respond. "In your testimony, you mentioned that yourself and Daniel regularly hung out underneath this bridge, is that correct?" A picture of the aforementioned bridge blew up on the big screen across the room. Daniel watched as the jurors' eyes flicked down to their own personal ipads in front of them to analyse the photograph.

"Yes"

"So, what are we talking then, two or three times a week?" Paul knew what he was doing. He was a cat playfully toying with the mouse.

"Umm nah, not that regularly."

"So, how often then? What do you mean when you say, let me just check my notes-" Paul glanced down theatrically. He didn't need any kind of reminder, "-regularly?" James spoke quietly into the microphone.

"Maybe two or three times". It was so quiet that the judge asked him to repeat himself.

"Two or three times", he announced into the microphone again. Daniel smiled as the familiar chatter flooded throughout the courthouse, reverberating from the walls with the shock. Only this time, it felt like the soundwaves carried a ring of hope which they hadn't birthed before.

"Two or three times ever? In almost six years of friendship?" Paul announced with a sense of incredulity. "I wouldn't call that regular James". His voice was that of a disappointed teacher. He didn't say anything in response but his eyes dropped to the ground.

"Did you go to the bridge with other friends James?" He nodded, "Yes, occasionally".

"And what is occasionally in your world then James? Once in a blue moon"? He smirked and it felt like he was teetering on the edge of bullying.

"A couple of times" James responded.

"Hmm, so occasional and regular are interchangeable it seems". It wasn't a question but he left a pause on the other end as if waiting for James to bite at his bait.

"Did your other friends know about this loose brick in the bridge? The one where you claim Daniel and yourself used to hide alcohol and drugs?"

"Some of them did yeah".

"So, this loose brick wasn't so secret after all then". It still wasn't a question but this time Paul left no time for James to respond. He pulled up a video onto the screen.

"We have done some surveillance on this specific bridge where the murder weapon and bloodied t-shirt was found. The video you are about to see is a time-lapse of twelve hours from 9pm on a Saturday night to 9am on Sunday morning". The video started to play and as it did, the jury watched on as tens of people wandered through under the bridge. The video lasted two minutes and 32 seconds and throughout that time, Paul didn't say a word. He stood and watched the clip, occasionally flickering his eyes back to the jury to gauge their reaction. Daniel's eyes lay fixated on James. When the clip finished and the screen went black, Paul spoke.

"On an average Saturday night, like the one filmed here, we counted forty-six people pass through under this bridge in this time frame. Forty-six".

"So, my question to you James Hunter, is, what makes you think it was Daniel who placed the murder weapon and bloodied t-shirt behind the brick that night? Can you really be sure that it was him and not one of several other people who walk through that same bridge?" James looked up, a brokenness emulating from behind his eyes.

"It's just where we kept things when we went there so it would make sense for him to use it as a hiding place".

"The two times you went there over the duration of six years, Daniel and yourself placed some weed behind that brick. It seems highly likely to me that in the countless other nights when you and Daniel did *not* venture down to that bridge, that other people could too have used that brick for their own personal use. If we replicate forty-six people every night over the course of six years, do you know how many people we get passing through under that bridge?" James shook his head.

"We get 100740. Do you think it's possible James, that one of these other 100740 people may too have found and used that brick as a stashing place?" James couldn't help but nod. Daniel smiled. It finally felt like they stood a chance. Perhaps taking a gamble on Paul hadn't been the worst idea after all. James sat up straight and leaned his body closer towards the microphone. He was not someone to easily make a fool out of. He was surprisingly sure of himself.

"I just don't think those 100740 people also their finger prints on the murder weapon and the victim's blood on the t-shirt". James narrowed his eyes at Paul, the way Daniel had seen him do with teachers who had tried to make him feel small or stupid or incompetent over the years. Paul retaliated quickly, determined not to let his comment take up space for long.

"We have already proven that the knife could have been handled using gloves." He paused and turned to face the jury, no longer solely addressing James.

"It seems to me that the planting of evidence in this place is a pathetic attempt to frame my client, Daniel Draker, for a crime he did not commit". Daniel felt a growing pit in his stomach. He indeed wanted doubt to be cast over the credulity of the story. But the idea of framing was a leap, he thought. It seemed far too fictional to be believed. Daniel resented Paul for planting that seed in amongst the others. It seemed far too messy.

"Ladies and gentleman of the jury, it is clear to me that my client, Daniel Draker is being used as a scapegoat in this case. It would be wrong for me to hypothesise who he is acting as a scapegoat for but it seems someone who knows him well enough to plant evidence as they have done." Again, he paused and, in that silence, Daniel wanted to strangle him.

"There is simply not enough evidence for you to conclude beyond all reasonable doubt that Daniel Draker is guilty of this crime. I urge you to consider the inconsistencies of the witness statements when you are deliberating your verdict. You simply cannot afford to send a young boy to prison with these niggling doubts at play".

Daniel looked over to the jury. He wanted to climb inside their minds and tamper with their thoughts. He wanted to soften the edges of their memories from the trial. He glanced back over towards the overweight man and noticed his eyes looked darker than before. His body seemed heavier, arms taxing on his torso. Daniel imagined all of the details of the case slowly seeping through his skin and nestling into his bones. He wondered how long the trauma would lull inside him after the case was finished. Would it lay dormant and erupt in moments of stress? Or would it fizzle away, never to be felt again? Would this man carry the weight of this case for the rest of his life? Would it weave and ebb into choices he makes? Would it change him? Daniel felt a deep ache settle at the back of his mind. This trial had changed him and he wished more than anything that he could take it all back.

The courthouse flooded out onto the streets just after 3:30pm. Daniel was piled back into the van with the shackles placed firmly all over his body. When he finally returned back to the prison, he was escorted back into the holding room and waited patiently for the strip search to be finished. After it was done, he was given back his prison jumpsuit to change back into and he could feel the feeling of anonymity return to his bones. He wasn't anyone inside here. No one cared about him in the way they did out there and Daniel wasn't sure if that was for better or worse. He was led through to the canteen where the noise was piercing and it reminded of him of being back in school. He found an empty seat and plonked himself down, tucking into the sausage and mash he had been given. Daniel loved prison food. He had never experienced so much 'home-cooked' food in all his life and he felt so grateful to be having a warm meal every evening when before his usual dinner was a bowl of cheerios. He sat in silence, munching his food down and praying that no one would sit next to him. Not tonight. He just needed to be alone with his own thoughts.

Day Three: The defense

Daniel didn't sleep last night. He lay, still, staring blankly up at the ceiling above him. He couldn't help but wonder if prison ceilings were one of the most studied in the world. It had to be a close call between that and Sistine chapel. Daniel felt the emptiness of the prison was more to his style anyway.

Today was his day to defend himself, his opportunity to speak his truth, if only he chose to take it. But he knew he was in too deep now. The web of lies was complex. It was an intricate spiral made from omissions of truths and small white lies which had grown faster than he could have ever imagined. There was no going back now and deep down he knew that. Still, today was his only chance to defend himself from a lifetime behind these four walls. He was willing to at least give it a shot. All he needed to do was to convince those twelve men and women that he was not the monster they thought he was. He needed them not to believe the lies he had told them.

A guard came and knocked loudly on his door, telling him to get up and grab his towel. He was elated to know he was able to have a shower this morning. The water had been busted the last few days and it hadn't set him with his best foot forward for the trial. But today, he inhaled deeply as the luke-warm water poured over his body. The steady stream was intermittently broken by bursts of scolding hot power followed by seconds of icicles pounding his body. He rubbed his hand through his hair and lathered his body in soap, scrubbing it as hard as he could, with the dying hope that a new man might appear beneath.

Once he had been strip searched, he put on his clean suit and was piled into the van to drive to the courthouse. It was the third day of the same journey and there was a routine familiarity to it now which brought Daniel some comfort. *Right, left, left. Pause at the temporary traffic lights and watch the people darting in and out of the coffee shops, always in such a hurry. Straight, right, right and straight along the road until the court house appeared.* It was approximately an eighteen-minute drive, depending on how caught they got by the lights. It was in those eighteen minutes where Daniel would allow his mind to drift, give way to the fantasy of life again, the words of 'not guilty' ringing in his ears. For those eighteen minutes in the morning, the possibility of all of that somehow seemed feasible. The eighteen-minute return journey at the end of the last two days hadn't held that same hope no matter how hard Daniel had tried to find it. He prayed that today might hold a new promise.

The van pulled up outside the courthouse and the flashing cameras began before he had even opened the car door. He imagined the headlines yet again; *Murderer shows no signs of remorse. Cold-blooded killer looks calm and content.* If only they could hear the inside of his head, he thought. If only they knew how his life had forever been riddled by a guilt which had never been his to carry. His father's fury, his mother's addiction, and then there was Lily. And how he had never been able to truly

187

protect her from Dad or Mum or Ayla. At least that was, not until now.

He walked purposefully into the building; eyes glued to the ground as he did. He was met by Paul, who looked weary despite the upbeat persona he was forcing. He held a cup of coffee in one hand and some papers in the other and had a half-grin painted across his face. Daniel couldn't help but think he must have slept more soundly than Paul last night. His mind drifted to what Paul ate for dinner and he somehow doubted it was anything as good as his sausage and mash. They walked into the court room together and for the first time since the trial had begun, Daniel looked at all of his family members in turn. He stared directly into his dad's eyes, regretting that he had insisted on him being here. Daniel gave him that same stare he had been given all those years ago; the glare of a hidden secret. Gavin did not give him anything back, not an inch. He then turned to his mum and softened his eyes. He couldn't help but feel proud of how far she had come, of the progress she had made. He blamed her for so much of who he had become, but in that moment, he felt an outpouring of love for all of the things she had done right. She had been to visit him every single week since he had been remanded and Daniel had been shocked at every visit. He had watched as a brightness returned to her face, as her hollow cheeks filled out again and as the twinkle returned to her eye. He watched every week as she healed herself back into a human and begin the learnings of what it meant to be a mother. His gaze then finally rested onto Lily. They locked eyes and hers brimmed with tears, threatening to explode at any given moment. She couldn't bear to see her big brother where he was. He gave her a nod to reassure her and held his chin high in the air, prompting her to mirror him. She smiled. They had always been a team after all.

Daniel took his seat next to Paul and Lily kept her eyes fixed firmly on the back of his head. The gallery rose from their seats as the judge confidently strolled in and took his position behind the lectern. The jury filed in, coffee in hand and a fresh focus behind their eyes. They would have fallen asleep last night with only one explanation in their minds. They would have dozed off with an assurance of guilt. But when their alarm rudely awoke them from a deep slumber, a settling of dust would have rested on their shoulders; a feeling just heavy enough not to ignore. A sprinkling of doubt. Daniel and Paul both knew that they had to help that seed flourish in every way they could.

The first witness was called to the stand. His name was Fazihma Shah. He worked at the fish and chips shop. As he pottered up to the stand, Daniel was struck by how small and frail he looked. He had never realised how old he was until now. Faz held up his right hand by his side and made his affirmation to the courthouse.

"I do solemnly, sincerely and truly declare and affirm that the evidence I shall give shall be the truth the whole truth and nothing but the truth"; he had the voice of a good man, Daniel thought. Faz spoke with a sincerity which echoed throughout the room. Unlike the others, he had not felt any twisted anticipation about being in the limelight today. He had spent over twenty-five years working hard to build his business and he deeply feared about the impact all of this would have; there is such a thing as bad press after all and he didn't want to see how it unfolded.

Paul begun,

"Fazihma, please can you state to the jury how you know my client Daniel Draker", Faz looked towards Daniel,

"Yes, he often comes into the chippy. He's been a customer for some years now".

Daniel worried that the testimony of the man who worked the fish and chip shop didn't seem quite as compelling as the friends of ten years who had testified against him just yesterday but Paul could only work with the hand he had been dealt. In terms of witness statements, this was the best he could get.

"On 17th February 2024, did you see Daniel Draker?"

"Yes, he came in and brought some food".

"And what time was this?"

"I would say between midnight and one in the morning".

"I see. And how long was Daniel in your shop would you say?"

He paused,

"I can't be certain but there was a couple of people in the queue ahead of him so maybe about twenty minutes or so?"

"Understood", Paul continued.

"And how did Daniel present to you whilst he was in your shop?"

"He seemed normal, I guess. He was swaying a little and he had clearly had quite a lot to drink".

"And what about his clothes? How did they appear to you?"

"I didn't notice anything. He looked completely normal to me"

"So, no blood stains or mud or anything out of the ordinary?"

"Not that I noticed no". Paul wished for him to just deliver a simple 'no'. He didn't want to leave any room for doubt amongst the jury.

"So when you saw Daniel on the night of the 17th February, the night that Ayla was murdered, he didn't present any differently to you than normal?"

"No, not at all". That was better, Paul thought.

"Ladies and gentlemen of the jury. I ask that you cast your eyes to the post-mortem on the screen in front of you". The screen blew up the post-mortem document in big writing for all of the courthouse to see. "The time of death clearly states that Ayla died between midnight and 1am". He left a beat for the facts to sink in before continuing, "It is simply not possible for Daniel Draker to have murdered Ayla Stevens whilst he was simultaneously in a fish and chip shop over half a mile away from the scene of the crime". He paused. "It is clear that Daniel Draker has a strong alibi for where he was when the murder was taken place. This alibi is supported by Fazihma's account. This is compelling evidence which rules out Daniel as a potential suspect for this case". Paul mustered all of his authority as he spoke. He knew how important it was for everything to go right; there was simply no room for error on this case. Daniel glanced over to the jury and noticed them jotting down some notes. He felt a wave of excitement rush through him, knowing that they at least now had something else to consider. Daniel felt a rush of relief that he had got chicken and chips that night. He mulled over how this could be the piece of evidence which saves him.

"Thank you Fazihma, that will be all". Faz briefly locked eyes with Daniel from across the room. He didn't know what to believe. Faz had always though Daniel to be a good kid after all. And the timings didn't match up, he knew that. But Faz had seen many good kids make bad choices over the years. He had watched as alcohol wrapped its noose around the necks of countless young lads who washed their future away with the temptation of 'just one more'. He had seen drunken brawls end in tragedy. He had heard clicks of car keys which should have stayed locked. He had heard screeching tyres which just couldn't stop. Faz wasn't sure what to believe any more. His faith in humanity was wearing thin.

John took a couple of paces up and down the floor before even opening his mouth, as if seizing up his prey.

"My name is John Seines and I am representing the Crown Prosecution Service. Would you rather me call you Fazihma or Faz?"

"Faz is fine", he replied, and his shoulders fell half a centimeter from his ears.

"I hear you have a successful chicken and chips shop on the high-street Faz, is that correct?"

"Yes, it is". Daniel tried not to smirk at the blatantly obvious attempt to flatter Faz. Surely Faz could see through the bullshit too, he thought.

"How many customers would you say you get on average in a day?" Faz scratched his head and his eyes looked to the ceiling as he tried to calculate the answer.

"I'd say somewhere between one-hundred and two-hundred".

"Wow. That certainly is a lot of people coming in and out of your shop."

"What age would you say is typical of your customers?"

"All ages sir. Everyone loves chicken". He smiled, a soft proud smile for the business he had built.

"Let me be more specific then. On a typical Friday or Saturday night, between the hours of 11pm to 2am, what would you say the typical age of your cliental is?'

"That's when the young'uns are out, I guess so maybe 18-25." Faz had loosened up now and the tension had almost released from his shoulders completely.

"So, by your own admission then Faz. On February 17th 2024, a Friday night, your typical clients between 11pm and 2am would have been primarily 18-25 years olds". Faz nodded.

"Yes".

"And you don't personally know Daniel Draker, do you"? Faz shook his head,

"No, I don't know him personally but he often came into my shop. He'd mostly come after a night out with his friends. He was a good lad I thought, never gave me any trouble". Daniel wanted to tell Faz that he was still a good lad, that nothing had changed, not really.

"Faz, I put it to you that you might well have mis-identified Daniel on the night of the murder. After all, there were several young men coming in and out of your chicken shop between those hours. How can you be sure that it was Daniel in your shop at the time you claim?"

"I'm good with faces", Faz responded without flinching.

"And times? Are you good with times too Faz? Because Daniel may well have been in your chicken shop that night yes. But can you be sure that he was there between midnight and 1am?"

"I'm pretty sure yes".

"Pretty sure? Pretty sure is not sure Faz. And in a case of this seriousness, we need you to be absolutely sure." Another silence. "Do you have CCTV in your shop Fazihma?"

"I do usually yes but it was out for a couple of weeks at the time she-" he took a breath in, "at the time she was killed. So, I don't have any CCTV from that night, I told the police that".

"Okay so there is no CCTV evidence placing Daniel Draker in your chicken shop that night", he pushed on.

"How do your customers pay for their food?"

"Cash" he followed it up quickly, "I'm old school like that". No one was falling for it but John didn't care if Faz was avoiding taxes. In fact, the lack of card transactions played into his hand perfectly in this particular case.

"Okay so we have no CCTV evidence and no card transactions to place Daniel at your shop at the time that he is claiming to be there", he turned to face the jury. "The only 'evidence' that we have placing Daniel Draker at Mr Shah's chicken shop that night is the eye-witness testimony from one man. One. I'd like to take this moment to remind the ladies and gentlemen of the jury about the unreliability of eyewitness testimony. In fact, eyewitness testimony was responsible for over half of all wrongful convictions in the last year alone". He paused and turned to face back towards Faz.

"Faz, I am not saying this to discredit yourself. I am sure you have the right intentions. But it is very important that we are aware of our own capacity for human error. Are you absolutely certain that Daniel Draker was in your shop between the hours of midnight and 1am on 17th February 2024 Faz?"

"I'm sure he was there that night. I'm certain of it." A pause. "But I guess I can't be exactly certain of the time. It might have been slightly earlier or later than that, I'm not sure". John started to pace again then. But not like an animal seizing up his prey this time, but rather a predator biding his time to indulge in his kill. He turned to face the jury.

"I put it to the jury that Daniel may well have gone into Faz's shop that night to buy chicken nuggets and chips. But I place serious doubt on the timeline of this. Daniel eating chicken the night of Ayla's murder is not an alibi. It is, at most, the actions of a man with no remorse for the murder of a seventeen-year-old girl". There was an uncomfortable silence fizzling in the air.

'Thank you Mr Shah, no further questions". Fazihma was excused from the stand and he looked frazzled as he shuffled back towards his seat. It was almost as if John had placed a seed of doubt in his own mind as well as the rest of the jury. That didn't bode well.

The next witness was called to the stand only minutes after Faz had taken his seat in the gallery. The pace felt faster than it had yesterday and Daniel begged for a moment to breathe. The next defense witness was the blood splatter expert. Her name was Dr Fischer and she walked with far more purpose than Faz had. She looked like someone who had been told she was capable from a very young age. She moved with a confidence of a woman in a man's profession; a brashness which may have been deemed cocky if she didn't have the PHD and ten years' experience to go along with it. She wore a sparkling diamond on her ring finger. A statement which screamed, *I have it all.*

"Please state your name and occupation to the jury," Paul begun after she had made her affirmation.

"I am Dr Mary Fischer and I am a blood spatter analyst". She looked far too young to be named Mary, Daniel mused.

"Are you the person who analysed the blood splatters on the t-shirt found beneath the bridge?"

"Yes, I am"

"For the jury, please give a summary of what you discovered when you completed this analysis"

"Certainly. Blood appears differently under the microscope depending on the length of time it has been soaking there. Ayla Stevens blood was found on the t-shirt that I examined" she paused, "however, the blood molecules suggest to us that the blood was printed onto the fabric at a later time than the post-mortem results indicate that Ayla Stevens died".

There was a hushed silence as everyone tried to piece together exactly what this meant.

"So, what are you claiming?" Paul chimed in.

"I am telling you that the timings do not add up. The blood was soaked into the shirt hours after the timeframe of her death." Paul nodded.

"So, to clarify, are you saying that the t-shirt which was found under the bridge was not worn at the time of Ayla's death?"

"Yes, in my professional opinion, the t-shirt was not present at the time of the murder itself".

Daniel glanced back over to the jury. It didn't really feel like enough. He could see a flash of confusion splash across their faces but it looked tainted somehow. He prayed that perhaps it was just enough to sow just a seed of doubt in their heads. That was all that was needed after all, a fraction of doubt to unsettle the certainty, a spark which couldn't be put out.

"Thank you, Dr Fischer. No further questions". She smiled as she nodded her head ever so slightly.

"Hi Dr Fischer, my name is John Seines". He smiled softly towards her.

"Dr Fischer, I understand it was you who undertook the examination of Daniel's t-shirt which was found with the murder weapon?"

"Objection", Paul rose to his feet, "We can't be certain that was Daniel's t-shirt". John smiled sarcastically, a smile which suggested his goading had worked just as he had planned.

"I apologise judge. It's just the exact same t-shirt that Daniel was wearing that night as seen on the CCTV outside of the pub and is covered in his DNA as well as Ayla's blood as Dr Fischer examined." He paused, "I am more than happy to retract my statement to *a* t-shirt if Mr Paul Grange would prefer".

"Overruled. The statement is fine".

"Apologies Dr Fischer. As I was saying, was it yourself who undertook the examination of Daniel's t-shirt?"

"Yes, it was". She responded.

"Since neither myself nor the rest of the jury are blood splatter experts, can you please explain this process in layman's terms for us?"

"Certainly". She stood up straight in the stand, exuding a confidence which teetered on cocky. "We can tell a lot about how someone died through looking at the blood splatters. For example, the shape of the bloodstain pattern depends on the force that was used to propel the blood. This can help us in determining the murder weapon that was used". She paused and turned her body towards the jury. "However, in some cases there are overlapping stains which can obscure the detail of the patterns, as was the case during this analysis".

"I see, so please tell us what you were able to confirm from your analysis?"

"Due to the high amount of blood and overlapping stains on the t-shirt, we were not able to conclude the force by which the instrument was used. But we were able to place the time somewhere between 3am and 4am. This did not align with time of death provided by the post-mortem".

"I see", he paused.

"And so, from this, it was concluded that Daniel was not wearing this t-shirt at the time of death?".

"That's correct".

"How many murder cases have you worked on Dr Fischer?" The change of pace clearly took her by surprise and she leaned back into her chair.

"Umm, around seventy I would say, at a guess that is".

"I see. And in any of these cases, have there been times in which the murderer returns to the crime of the scene after the event?" She nodded. "In one or two perhaps yes".

"I put it to you Dr Fischer that this could be an explanation for the discrepancy in your findings and those of the post-mortem. I put it to you that Daniel murdered Ayla Stevens in the park that night and left her die". He paused, "Perhaps then realising that he may get caught, I believe he returned to the crime of the scene a couple of hours after she had died to remove the murder weapon and I believe that is when the soaking of the t-shirt occurred. Would you say this is a possible hypothesis Dr Fischer, based on the evidence you have seen?"

She nodded. "It could be yes". John turned to face the jury then.

"It is clear to me that the discrepancy between the time of death on the post mortem and the time at which Ayla's blood soaked into Daniel's t-shirt is nothing more than the result of a man desperately trying to cover his tracks, frantically trying to hide evidence. Thank you, Dr Fischer, I have no more questions".

Dr Fischer walked down from the lectern. She still walked with that same sense of pride which seemed somewhat misplaced considering what had happened, Daniel thought. But then again, she wasn't there to take sides, she wasn't there to convince. She was an expert before the trial and she would still be an expert after.

The judge rose to his feet then.

"The time is 12:30pm. There will be an hour lunch break and court will resume promptly at 1:30pm". Daniel could feel the butterflies flock to his stomach. He would have to wait for a whole hour. It felt cruel. Daniel could feel an anger towards the judge bubble away inside. Paul on the other hand, appeared relieved to have an hour's respite. He sat down next to Daniel at the wooden table in the break room where they had been led by the security guards.

"Nothing beats a ham and cheese sandwich," he announced with a wink as he unwrapped his tin foil and folded it neatly into a small triangle. Daniel took tiny bites of the tuna sandwich he had been given. He felt like he could throw up at any given moment but he knew he needed to eat, if nothing else just to pass the time. The hour dragged on and on and Daniel felt tears brim in his eyes by the time they were finally called back into the courtroom. Everyone scuttled back into their seats just before 1:30pm. No one was risking missing the end of today's show. Daniel scanned the room and was sure that it was busier now than it had been that morning. This time he avoided looking directly at his family. He needed to be strong for this and he was frightened he might completely break if he saw Lily's tears.

The judge entered the room and everyone rose to their feet.

"Thank you for all being on time. The defense has one final witness for the day. Can I please call Mr Daniel Draker up to the stand". The silence was deafening. Paul had practically begged him not to do it. Everyone he had spoken to had told him it was a bad idea. They had warned him how the story so quickly can be twisted and pulled in all directions. But Daniel had stayed firm. He wanted to be able to look the jurors in the eye and promise them that he hadn't murdered Ayla Stevens. He needed that peace, if only for himself.

Shaking, he rose from his seat and made his way up to the lectern. He didn't look at anyone as he did. His mind was laser-focus. He pictured Ronaldo, walking up to the penalty spot but he knew that this was not to be his crowning moment of glory. His victory, if indeed it came, would be laced in a far more somber silence.

When he finally reached the lectern, he stood in place, his head high, his shoulders broad. He confidently held up his hand and stared towards the jury, scanning all of their faces.

"I do solemnly, sincerely and truly declare and affirm that the evidence I shall give shall be the truth the whole truth and nothing but the truth" He willed them to lock eyes with him. He wanted them to bear witness to his rawness. Only one member did. He had shaggy blonde hair and was a little overweight. His glare was forceful, anaylsing every inch of Daniel. He looked like the sort of guy who was probably bullied during secondary school but since leaving, he had found a solid group of friends who had allowed him to express himself. He must have only been about twenty-five. Daniel willed him to look deep into his soul, he needed this man, this one man, to see him for who he truly was.

Paul's body began to tremor. He had woken up this morning in a frenzy, telling his wife over and over again that he had told Daniel not to do it. His wife had given him a hug and reassured him that he had tried his best and whatever would be would be. She said she would have dinner waiting for him when he got home and he would be able to tuck in his children after their bath time. He had left the house with stress bleeding into his psyche, fear gripping his stomach and twisting it in knots. He begun, his voice shaking,

"Daniel, can you please tell us what happened on the night of February 17th, in your own words". Daniel nodded and took a deep breath. This was it. He darted his eyes over to Lily and immediately wished he hadn't; tears were already streaming from her face. What a mess this was.

"I was out with some friends for my birthday at the Red Dragon. We had a few drinks and chatted and that you know, just a normal night I guess". He paused and Paul nodded at him to continue, "And then afterwards, I thought we might go out, like I was dead keen on going clubbing but no one was really up for it so I called it a night". Another pause. "So, I walked to Faz's to pick up some chicken and chips for me and Lily and then I went home. That was it".

"Was Ayla Stevens there that night?" Paul prompted. He knew he had to tease out some of the hard truths early on. He had told Daniel that if he insisted on going on the stand, then he would have to use the time explain his side of the story before the cross examination tried to derail it. It was important to acknowledge some of the events so that it wouldn't look suspicious to the jury.

"Yes, she came to see Lily". There was a slight uncertainty in the air as the words left his mouth and Daniel couldn't work out what he had said wrong. He noticed John furiously scribbling on the piece of paper in front of him.

"Did you two speak much during the night?"

"Not really no, just at the end when, well, you know…" he trailed off. Paul picked up the baton quickly, hoping no one had noticed it slip,

"When you and Ayla had your disagreement outside yes. Tell us what happened after that?" Daniel admired his choice of wording and wondered whether any of the jury would fall for it.

"We went our separate ways. I went to the chicken shop and grabbed some food and then went home. I don't know where she went because I didn't see her again. The next morning was the first I heard about anything, when the police knocked on our door". *Look earnest. Look sincere. Look human.* Paul had been very clear about his instructions. Juries want to see people react how they think they should react. They want to see the movie expectation because it's something they can fathom. But it was hard with so many eyes glaring into him, so many faces tracing his every expression.

"So, let's be clear Daniel. You're saying that after you left the pub, you went to the chicken shop. Which, ladies and gentleman of the jury, has been confirmed by Fazihma himself. And after you had picked up the chicken, you went directly home".

Daniel nodded, "That's correct yes".

"And you didn't leave your house until the next morning when the police arrived?"

"That's correct". Paul nodded,

"How did you feel towards Ayla Stevens Daniel?"

"Nothing really, we weren't really friends but I didn't mind her. I just wanted her to treat Lily right".

"And how did you feel when you found out she had died?" Daniel glanced over to the jury,

"I was in shock, I guess. I just couldn't believe it". He paused, "And I was worried for Lily. I knew how much she loved her and I didn't want her to feel sad".

"Are you responsible for the death of Ayla Stevens Daniel?"

"No, I'm not. I promise I had nothing to do with it".

"Thank you, Daniel, no further questions". Daniel took another deep breath and desperately tried to stop his sweating. He had always mocked the teachers who had told him 'Public speaking' was an important life skill but it turns out, it was the most important of them all. It would soon determine whether he had a free life or an imprisoned one.

John rose to his feet then and slowly walked to the center of the floor. Daniel could feel the butterflies gently floating inside him, promising that they would never land.

"Hi Daniel, I'm John." He left an uncomfortable pause and Daniel wondered whether he was expected to respond.

"Daniel, let me start with the statement you made in your testimony", Daniel's mind flashed back to the image of him hunched over the table, furiously scribbling notes.

"You said that Ayla had come to see Lily at the pub, is that correct?"

"Yes"

"But it was your birthday that night, is that correct?"

"Yes"

"I would imagine that frustrated you?" Daniel paused,

"Umm, I don't know". Daniel knew it was the wrong answer as soon as the words left his mouth. John didn't falter, the words rolling from his tongue as if he had every possible response programmed.

"From the testimonies that we have heard, it seems it was no secret that you and Ayla didn't get along. And then she shows up on your birthday when you are celebrating with all of your friends. Not only that, but she came to see your sister, Lily, whose relationship you did not approve of". Daniel looked up, confused as to whether he was meant to comment during the silence. He had been expecting more questions than this.

"Did their relationship upset you, Daniel?" His eyes glanced around, desperate to find some answers from across the room. The courtroom looked fuzzy, the world pixelating around him as if this moment in time was still loading somehow.

"Yeah, I didn't like her". *But I didn't kill her.* He muttered only in his head. He glanced over to Paul who had his eyes locked on Daniel but his body hunched towards the ground.

"After the pub had closed that night, you physically assaulted Ayla outside of the pub, as was captured on CCTV here". The video started playing out again for the courthouse to see. Daniel watched on, praying for a different ending. *Unclench your fist. Don't do it. Don't hit her. It's not worth it.* Daniel knew why John had wanted to replay that clip. It was the piece of evidence that the jury would surely circle back to when there was uncertainty about his character. It was certainly the moment he circled back round to every night in his nightmares. He was the man who hit women. That stroke in his character could never be unpainted. Regardless of everything else they would debate on; this would remain steadfast in their minds eye.

"This, uh, 'disagreement', as Paul so kindly put it. What triggered it?"

"I can't remember", Daniel replied without a moment of hesitation. John theatrically recoiled, his hand reaching up to touch the side of his head.

"You can't remember?" He announced, "It is an incredibly violent outburst not to be able to remember the reason for it Daniel." Again, he waited, testing Daniel's ability to withstand the silence. "It looks as if Ayla said something which riled you up Daniel, is that right?"

"I can't remember", he repeated, with a slight venom in his voice this time.

"Are you and your sister close Daniel?" The question caught him off guard and he instantly began to shuffle his feet as Lily was mentioned.

"Yes, we are. She's like my best mate". Daniel glanced over to Lily as he said it but her eyes were fixated on the ground in front of her. She looked so small sat next to Gavin. He felt sick seeing them sat next to each other.

"After you punched Ayla, were you worried about what Lily might think? I mean, you had physically assaulted her girlfriend for seemingly no reason, or at least a reason you can't even remember. The idea of explaining that to your little sister must have been pretty daunting, yes?"

Daniel sighed. He knew how it looked. The perfect storm.

"Yes, I guess I was".

"But the thing is Daniel, is you never did have to explain why you did that to Ayla after all did you? Because Ayla wasn't alive long enough to tell Lily what had happened. Ayla was murdered before she could tell Lily what kind of a monster you are". John stared at Daniel, his eyes piercing through the short distance between them. He believed in Daniel's guilt so surely.

"You killed Ayla that night, didn't you? You realised that Ayla would tell everyone what had happened and you couldn't risk Lily finding out. So, you didn't have a choice. You had to kill her before she could speak. You followed her home that night and murdered her in the park. You left her dying on the forest floor and then hid your bloody clothes and the knife before going back home and falling asleep with your sister sleeping in the next-door room, oblivious to the nightmare that was about to unfold".

"That's not true", Daniel weakly muttered. He offered no reason as to why it wasn't. Paul looked towards the floor. The truth itself wasn't enough. The claim of truth certainly wasn't.

"I want to believe you Daniel, I really do, but here's why I can't," he paused and raised his voice ever so slightly.

"You clearly had a deep hatred for Miss Ayla Stevens, as evidenced by your own admission and texts between you and your friends. You violently assaulted Ayla Stevens that night on the 17th February outside of the Red Dragon. Your fingerprints are on the murder weapon. Her blood is on your t-shirt. You had a clear motive and clear means. So, if you're telling me that you didn't murder Ayla Stevens that night, I think you owe the jury something more tangible than *but it wasn't me*". Daniel gulped. He hated the way John made him look. He hated being called a liar. But he had nothing else to say.

"But I didn't kill her. I promise I didn't".

"Unfortunately, Daniel, we know that you persistently lying throughout interviews with the police in relation to this case. Your promises do not hold any weight whatsoever". This time he didn't wait for Daniel to respond. He didn't wallow in the silence.

"No more questions, thank you". Daniel wanted to shout at him. He wanted to drag his name through the dirt. How dare he paint him out to be such a monster.

He slumped down from the box and back over towards his chair. He looked over to the man in the jury with the shaggy hair and the tired eyes. He looked defeated. Daniel felt a wave of anger towards him. How dare he have the audacity to be tired from this. It was not his life in the balance. The judge rose and asked both Paul and John to the floor to give their closing statements. There was an air of finality about the way he said it. The gallery held their breath. John went first.

"Ladies and Gentlemen of the jury, it seems to be that you have a particularly easy job on your hands today. There is no doubt that Daniel Draker murdered Ayla Stevens on the 17th February 2024. He was a young man filled with rage who sought revenge on his sister's girlfriend. Let us call a spade a spade; this murder was a crime of hate. Through looking at all of the evidence which has been presented, it is clear that Daniel had a vengeful vendetta against Miss Ayla Stevens. On the night of the 17th February 2024, his anger reached boiling point when he savagely attacked Ayla outside of the pub, as seen on CCTV. Fearful of what his sister might think, Daniel then followed Ayla through the park that night, murdering her in the most callous and cruel fashion. He then took actions to cover his steps, hiding both the murder weapon and his bloodied clothes, showing no remorse for his actions. Daniel Draker a dangerous man who poses a risk to women everywhere. Daniel took Ayla's life from her when she was just seventeen years old. Her family deserves justice. Ayla deserves justice. You must find Daniel Draker guilty and give them all the closure they so painfully deserve". He spoke with such eloquence. There was an eerie silence after he finished in which it felt like no one wanted to breathe so as not to disturb it.

It was Paul's turn now. It seemed like an almost impossible act to follow. But he walked to the center of the floor, his eyes piercing. He addressed the jury.

"Ladies and gentlemen of the jury. Despite what Mr Seines claims, you have a very hard challenge indeed ahead of you. Mr. Seines has tried his best to create an unjust and untrue depiction of my client, Daniel Draker. But Daniel Draker is not a monster; he is just a boy. And more so, he is a boy who did not commit the crime of which he is being accused. There are simply far too many inconsistencies for you to find Mr. Daniel Draker guilty. With that seed of doubt still inside your head, it is your duty to find my client not guilty. I urge you not to rest on your duty". Another silence lingered after he had finished but it didn't seem as poignant as the last. Paul strode back over to his seat next to Daniel and let out a deep, relieving breath as he sat down. The judge spoke then in a bellowing and assertive voice. "Jury. You now have the job of reaching a unanimous verdict. Please consider all of the evidence which has been put before you. We will reconvene when a unanimous verdict has been reached". The scuffle of noise and the whispers of the public was like torture, a reminder of the world they belonged to. This was a mere snippet of their day, an anecdote for friends at a dinner party. The jury stood up and filed out in one single line and into a room filled with tea and coffee and snacks to keep them going. All of the evidence was splashed out across the table and they sat down having one on one conversations. Even now, small talk somehow still crept in; the rain pounding against the window being discussed as though it important.

Day Four: The verdict

When the guard woke Daniel early that morning, he forgot where he was for the first few moments. As if almost in a trance, it took him until his feet hit the ground for the coldness of the cell to engulf him. Like an electric current, it travelled up through his body, electrocuting him back to his reality.

He was escorted through to the shower room and felt the hot water cascade down his back, the water droplets effortlessly roll from his skin. He lathered himself in the soap and watched as the bubbles formed and burst. He rubbed his hands over his body and allowed the shame to swallow him as he did. He had once taken so much pride in the way he looked. He felt a crushing sense of loss as he felt his withered body in the shower. He closed his eyes and saw Ayla's body lying on the muddy floor, her collarbone protruding from beneath her skin. He thought how she would have loved that feature when she was living. But it wasn't so pretty now she was dead. No one spoke about her body anymore or the way it curved in all the right places. After all, dead girls aren't pretty.

After the shower, Daniel changed into his grey tracksuit. He sat on the edge of his bed and waited for the guard to knock back on his cell. Time slowed in his cell and he couldn't be sure how long he was sitting there. *Two.* He guessed. *Two knocks.* It was the same game he played every morning. It was usually two knocks, occasionally it was three. There was the grumpy guard named Frederik who only ever knocked a solitary once and it filled Daniel with unease when he heard it. And then there was that one time when Annie had knocked that happy, homely, tuneful knock and Daniel had burst into tears right there on the spot. *Rat-ta-ta-ta-tat, tat-tat.*

By the time the knock came, Daniel couldn't even remember to register how many knocks it was after all. It was time. He could feel his body jittering in the van on the way to the courthouse. He tried to slow down his thoughts but they pulsated through him like cancerous blood, worming their way into every corner of his body. When they finally pulled up to the courthouse, he saw Lily, Hayley and Gavin standing by the steps. It was a picture-perfect sight and Daniel couldn't help but register the irony. His parents hadn't showed up for him throughout his childhood, through all of the tears and fears and confusion, they hadn't been there. And yet, there would be journalists sympathetically asking them what went wrong and how their son turned out to be such a monster. He wondered if they would admit to their part in it all.

It had taken the jury five hours and six minutes to reach their verdict. In that time, they pondered independently and argued in unity. Each of their own lives leaking into their judgements. It was impossible for them not to. Philip was gay. Jeremy was rich. Ellie was poor. Charlotte had never learnt how to hate. Janine's boyfriend had punched her in the head when she didn't want to have sex with him after giving birth to their baby. Paul was tee-total and believed alcohol could make monsters out of men. Robert had been the monster. Their own lives had bred prejudice so deeply, it was part of who they were. How could they be expected to park it all to one side for a decision as important as this one?

Daniel sat in his chair at the table. Paul and he did not say a single word to each other. They sat and stared into the abyss, imagining a world in which 'not guilty' escaped the jurors' lips, in which there were gasps of outrage and confusion, in which there were camera crews surrounding Daniel's house for a few days before the big news story hit and he could silently fade into the background, forgotten in the best possible way. Daniel looked around and was amazed at how many people had stuck around all that time to hear the verdict. The thought of strangers caring so actively about one life bemused him. He wondered whether they cared about Ayla and her family and justice for them, or whether it was him they cared about. He wondered whether it would be her parent's relief they looked towards first or his despair. He imagined it would likely be the latter. Punishment is valued so much more highly than justice after all.

"The jury have reached their verdict. Foreperson, please stand", the judge requested.

"Based on the evidence you have heard throughout the course of this trial, how to you find Mr Daniel Draker on the offence of first-degree murder?"

The world stopped spinning in those seconds. There was a bubble expanding from within Daniel which grew so big, it shut out the rest of everything. He stood in a parallel universe, watching himself from above, desperately reaching in, trying with all of his might to pull him from his own body, to save him from his own mind.

"Guilty" a dagger shot through the bubble, bringing him back to his own reality. There was a clamor of noise, a yelp from Ayla's mother as she sobbed into the arms of her husband; pain and relief circling one another, seeping through into their veins. Paul rested his hand on Daniel's shoulder as the clutter of noise bounced around the room. Daniel stared directly at the ground, tears filling his eyes.

Part 3
The truth

Hayley

I woke up early today and walked over to the prison gates. It was a forty-two-minute walk from the house and I found the fresh air helped before my visits. I couldn't help but feel guilty as the sun soaked into my skin and the breeze whistled through the air as I walked. I knew Danny wouldn't be so lucky. It had been five years, three months and six days since the sentencing. A couple of weeks after the guilty conviction, Daniel had been called back into the courthouse for his sentencing. In those few weeks, a lot of people had lost interest in his misery. The courtroom was near empty and it felt awfully strange being there with Ayla's parents so close, without the buffer of strangers between us. Sure enough, swiftly after Dan had been convicted, the papers had found something else to scream about. Lily had told me there was still an active Facebook page named 'Justice for Ayla' which tended to focus on death threats towards our family instead of tributes towards her. The sentencing hearing hadn't lasted longer than twenty minutes. The judge focussed on the brutality of her death and on the supposed lack of remorse which Daniel had displayed. In the end, he was given a twenty-five-year sentence. Paul explained to me that since Daniel had been eighteen on the day of the murder, the judge was able to give him a harsher sentence than he would have if he had still technically been a juvenile. What a day to choose to kill someone I had thought.

I visited Dan almost every week. We would sit and chat and have a cup of tea. I would tell him about my job and he would tell me how proud he was of me for staying clean. He would tell me about the food he was given and how he was enjoying playing chess with a couple of the guys in there. We would never talk about the life which was wasting away with every day that passed. We never touched on the mistakes that had led him there nor the regrets that we both held so deeply within ourselves. And I never told the truth about what I had seen that night, the silhouette of a man I knew all too well.

It had been a normal day for me after all, the day of February 17th. I had woken up and messaged my dealers, desperate for a hit that would take me through to the next one. Because that's all life had been for me back then. Grasping for the artificial high, willing it to kill me because maybe then I wouldn't have to feel that crushing inevitable low that always followed. I still had enough crack for one more hit so I pierced the needle through my skin and felt my entire energy shift. I knew it was Danny's birthday that day and I knew that I had promised him that I would be sober. But I also knew that nothing was more important in that moment than the high I so desperately needed.

It must have been years since I had been sober for Danny's birthday. On the first birthday he had after Gav had been put inside, I remember buying him a chocolate cake from the co-op down the road. We had sat around the table singing happy birthday and Danny was smiling the entire evening. I was so proud to be able to give him that. Late that night, I had knocked on his bedroom door to give him a kiss and wish him goodnight. I had walked in and Danny was holding the lighter beneath the palm of his hand, pain etched into every crevasse of his face. He dropped it immediately,

"I'm sorry," he had cried, tears streaming down his cheeks. I had run over towards him and the palm of his hand was red-raw. I rushed him into the bathroom and shoved his hand under the cold running water as he yelped out in pain.

"What were you doing Dan? Why would you do that?" I'll never forget the way his big brown eyes stared up at me, pain etched into them.

"I miss Dad". It was like a dagger into my stomach. It had been the first birthday I felt like everything had finally gone right and I couldn't bear the idea that this wasn't how it was supposed to be. I remember sneaking out that very night when the kids were fast asleep and tucked up in bed. That was the first night I got high. What kind of a mother does that make me?

I woke up around 10pm the night of the 17th. I had been out cold pretty much the entire afternoon. Neither Lils or Dan were in the house so I assumed they were both out celebrating at the pub. I had officially run out of smack now so I messaged both my dealers again. I almost immediately had received a message back from Ayla.

'Not until I get my money from the last two drops. I'm not fucking around with you anymore'. Shit. How did I forget again. But then another message came through.

'I might have to start charging your precious daughter for every fuck she gets'. I could feel my blood run cold. The control she wielded over Lily felt painfully familiar. My body lurched with a deep hatred. I wondered if Lily knew how she was being used. I somehow doubted it. When my hit arrived, I let the stillness wash over me and I didn't think about Lily or Dan or any of the things that actually mattered. I instead lay in front of the TV and flicked over to the cartoons that Dan used to love when he was little; I could feel the noise rattle through me and the colours on the screen blur into shapes I couldn't recognise. Two hours passed and the high was already wearing off. I texted my dealer again but there was no response. My body begun to shake with desperation and my brain started to feel like it was being scraped from the inside out, as if someone was digging their nails deeply into my psyche. My patience was wearing thin and the nausea was beginning to set in. I couldn't wait around any longer. Grabbing my coat, I stormed out into the icy night. The wind was howling and the street lamps flickered on and off as I strode along the pavement and towards the park. I knew that a few dealers were bound to be lurking around in the shadows. They each had their spots. I felt a resentment that I was having to go and find them when they usually came to me. As I walked deeper in through the trees, a

chill ran down my spine. It felt like I was being watched through the shadows. I walked deeper into the park, remembering that on the other side was a nightclub which was bound to have dealers lingering outside. The wind against my face was chilling but I continued pounding through the park, determined to get my fix.

It was then that I saw her. Lying flat on her back, blood gushing from her stomach. She was still gasping for air. I've read that in traumatic events, the world around you slow down and all of your senses become heightened. It didn't feel like that for me. I remember running towards her, my eyes flashing from side to side, frantically trying to absorb as much information as possible. I fell to my knees, collapsing next to her body. I didn't touch or try to help as the blood gushed out and onto the ground. I remember just staring at her as her life faded before my very eyes. I wish I could claim that I froze but my mind was alert and my decision not to try and help her was an active choice. I clocked the knife lying by her side. My mind rushed through a thousand thoughts, so many questions springing up and falling away just as quickly. I couldn't quite believe what I was seeing. I knew I should help. I knew my hands should be pressing against her body, desperately trying to keep the blood inside her. I knew I should be on the phone to the ambulance, begging them to get here as soon as possible. I knew I had the chance to save her life. And I knew I was choosing not to. I knew I was making a terrible mistake but I somehow couldn't bring myself to make a different one. Instead, I knelt next to her, silently watching her world fade away. As her eyes slowly rolled to the back of her head, and her gasps became less frantic, my mind centered back to the moment.

There were no more questions in my head. No more ought's or should's or could's. Because still, amongst all of the chaos and the mayhem surrounding me, was the overwhelming need for my fix. Nothing else mattered. I *was* my addiction back then. I pushed my hand into her pocket, fumbling for anything I could find. I grabbed the packets of pills and sachets of powder. I pulled out her house keys and left them on the ground next to her. There was around £200 and her phone along with the drugs and I stashed it all into my pocket. I stood up and brushed myself down before looking back up into the shadows amongst the trees.

There, less than five meters in front of me, he stood. As brazen and confident as the last time I had seen him all those years ago. His eyes locked into mine and he gave a wry smile because after all of this time, he knew that he was still in control. We both stared into each other as the fear and the guilt and the terror settled like dust that had never left. He stood his ground, firmly. So just like all those years ago, I turned and ran for my life.

I didn't stop running until I reached back home. I collapsed into the front door and let the gasps of trauma escape from within me. Fumbling in my pockets, I grabbed the drugs and stabbed the needle into my arm, feeling the instant release from reality. My soul floated up above me and my mind quietened. I managed to hobble back up the stairs and climb into bed, my eyes flickering open and shut, my head crashing onto the pillow.

It wasn't until the next morning when the reality of the night before started to sink in. I reached for the glass of stale water next to my bed as the grogginess settled. I dared not to close my eyes again as I feared seeing his steely eyes staring back. His smile teased and taunted me as I tossed and turned in the covers. I couldn't piece together the puzzle in my mind. Why had he been there? I knew he was a bad man, but I wouldn't in my wildest dreams have thought that Gav could kill Ayla. It didn't feel real. The questions fluttered around my room, desperately searching for a place to settle. Why had he been there? How did he know Ayla? Why would he kill her? Nothing added up. And everything was made worse in knowing that I couldn't even go to the police even if I had wanted to. Who would believe a washed-up druggie who had stolen from the dying girl? I lay in bed that day, wishing for the darkness to fold over the city, swaddling it like a blanket. I needed the secrecy of the night to paralyze me into a deep sleep.

I looked up at Danny across the table in the communal room with our cups of tea and shortbread sitting in front of us. I felt a deep aching. I wanted to apologise for the life I had given him. I wanted to tell him that I knew he didn't belong here, that I knew that it was Gav that had murdered that poor girl on that fateful night. I wanted to apologise for not being brave enough to tell the police about what I had seen. Everything had spiraled out of control so quickly and it felt like I had never even had the chance to breathe. Before I had known it, I was telling lies that I couldn't un-tell. All this time, I had always believed my addiction had controlled me.

The grasp of the heroin was the strongest pull I had ever felt. But as I sat there and looked into my son's beautiful eyes, the control from the heroin was now finally gone. And it dawned on me that the control from Gav still lurked. I wondered if it would ever leave me. Or whether his grip around my throat will always be there; it's as if his fingerprints are etched so deeply into my skin that they have nuzzled into my anatomy. And even when my skin sheds and new cells grow, the memory of his touch webs its way back into the new. As the seasons change and the years tick by, I become surer than ever that his power over me remains constant.

Gavin

Life is alright these days. I've settled into the mundaneness of it all. I woke up and had my cup of coffee and a cigarette as I sat and watched morning TV. I got dressed and went to work, chatting shit to the other lads I worked with who turned out to be alright blokes after all. They were mostly younger than me and hadn't made quite as many mistakes as I had but they still had lots of time for that. I'd sometimes pop into the pub after the shift and have a couple beers and watch the footie if it was on. And then I'd wander back home, half pissed and ready to flop into bed before doing it all again the next day. I didn't mind it. I remember growing up and thinking that one day my life might be extraordinary in some way. I guess that's what all kids think. Because that's what you're taught when you're young; the world is your oyster and that you can do or be anything you want. It's a load of bull. Maybe I wasn't always destined for this, but I sure as hell was never destined for anything great either.

I think about Danny often. I think about how he will spend more time behind bars than I ever had and I question the fairness in that fate. I wonder about how he is coping and whether he has made it in with the right crowd, the ones who will back him up if he ever finds himself in any trouble. I picture him surrounded by the blokes who I had been in with and think about how small and young he would look next to them; how easy it would be to pick on someone like him. I think about him every day. And I can't help but feel the guilt in knowing that he doesn't belong there. No one should be behind bars for a crime they didn't commit.

I replay the day back over in my head. I got the train down from Cardiff. Two hours and 51 minutes into Haverfordwest. The whole way there, I sat and thought about what I might say when I saw him. I imagined him opening up the front door and seeing my face and I imagined a grin escaping from him even if he didn't want it to. I imagined him inviting me to the pub and meeting all his friends and I imagined Lily being there to, chatting and smiling and pleased to see me. For two hours and 51 minutes, that is all I thought about. But then, when the train finally pulled in and I was stood outside the train station, the clouds drew over. I instead imagined him shutting the front door in my face. I imagined him blankly staring at me like he didn't even know who I was. I imagined Lily meeting my eye and bursting into tears of rage and anguish. And suddenly, I wasn't so sure about my plan after all. I had no reason whatsoever to think that they would want to see me. I hadn't spoken to either of them in years. Hell, I didn't even know if they all still lived in that same address. And God forbid I knocked on the door and Hayls opened it. That was the face of someone I certainly didn't want to see.

So instead, when the train pulled in, I didn't end up making my way to the house where we once lived. Instead, I walked around the town, popping into different pubs and soaking it all up. I sat at the bar and watched as young groups of friends piled in, laughing at nothing and being obnoxiously loud and I thought about how lucky they were. I watched on as they brought each other rounds and took the piss out of each other and danced so effortlessly from one conversation to the next. I wondered if they considered having friends to be a luxury. I wondered if they knew that good company and crappy beer was one of the few great joys in this life. I wondered if they would ever have the need for nostalgia in the way that I did.

As the night drew in and the darkness unfolded and the booze took hold, I found myself walking towards the park I used to take Danny and Lils to when they were kids and before everything seems to crumble. I stumbled around in the darkness and sat on the floor by a tree trunk as I drunk the remaining beers I had brought from the off-license. I must have dozed off there because I woke up a couple of hours later to the sound of branches cracking and muffled giggles. Half-drunk and in a complete daze,

I pulled myself up to my feet and starting to quietly walk towards the sound, not entirely sure what it was I was searching for.

It was then that I saw her; the curves of her face exactly the same as they had been the last time I had seen her. The waves in her hair fell so beautifully and her smile was magnetic. She looked so happy. My gorgeous Lily. I was overwhelmed with feelings of love and heartbreak all at once. She was with someone, a girl who looked older than her. They were laughing and it dawned on me that it could be the same girl she told me about back when I was in prison, the only chance I had ever been given to do something right and I had fucked it up all over again. I saw her lean in to kiss her, their lips touching slowly at first and then deeper and harder, as if they couldn't stop. It was as if they were the only two people in the world and nothing could take them away from the moment they were in. I saw the girl's hand work its way from tangled in Lily's hair, slowly touching down the crevasse of her back and begin to caress her inner thigh. I watched as Lily hiked her dress up and the girl started to kiss down her body.

I couldn't take it anymore. I looked away. I could feel the rage burning inside me and I was about to yell. It was rising in me like a volcano and I couldn't keep it in any longer. I felt so powerless and desperately wanted to stop what was happening. Just as I opened my mouth to shout, a scream came from somewhere else. It was the most blood-curdling thing I had ever heard. I looked back and I could see blood pouring from her stomach, Lily's hand on the knife plunged so deeply inside. I watched Lily stumble backwards and stare at what she had done. I saw the girl fall to the ground, grabbing her stomach as the blood gushed out. Lily dropped the knife on the floor and stood paralysed for a couple of seconds before turning back around. She looked over in my direction and paused for a second too long and I wondered whether she had spotted me lingering there. Her feet started running, her legs pounding the ground and before I knew it, she was gone, flying through the trees and disappearing into the darkness of the night. I stood silently in the shadows, watching as the girl just lay there, her life slowly fading away before my eyes.

I stood like a statue, frozen in a moment I should never have seen. I knew I should have gone over to help her. I could hear her rasping breath travel across the stillness of the night. But my feet felt as though they were glued to the ground. It didn't feel as though I was choosing not to help but more than I *couldn't* help. I've heard that in moments in trauma, people can become superhuman. The adrenaline can make mothers lift cars, it can help men fight sharks or run faster than they thought possible. But in that moment of trauma, I didn't become superhuman. I became sub-human. I didn't do anything in those crucial moments and I wonder who that makes me.

I stood in the eerie silence as the minutes passed by, with each one knowing that the girl's fate was being sealed firmer into the bed of the earth. It couldn't have been more than fifteen minutes later when I noticed a figure stumbling back towards the body. I held my breath. I expected to see Lily's sunken face returning amongst the darkness; a confusion etched deep in the furrow of her brow. A deep-rooted realisation that whatever she had done could not be taken back. I watched on as the figure fell to the floor and my stomach panged as I recognised the way she collapsed. It was my Hayley. My god, she looked like a shell of who she used to be. Her cheek bones protruded from her face and her frail body was swallowed by the huge coat she had on. She didn't seem to move at first, just slumped next to the corpse as her body heaved with fear and anguish. I wondered if she was praying; perhaps she had found God in the last ten years.

But then I watched as she frantically grabbed the drugs and money and the phone from the girl. Clearly, it had not been God she had found but rather the devil instead. She stood back up and we locked eyes across the shadows of the trees. I smiled at her. It gave me so much joy in knowing her life was just as fucked as mine was. Isn't it amazing what love can become. There was a time when I would have died for that girl and there I was, relishing in the mess her life had become. My dad's words echoed in my head: *tear the fuckers down with you.* I saw the fear envelope her body as all of the pieces fell into place. After all of this time, I still had control. I watched as she turned and ran through the trees, just like Lily had done.

I haven't been to visit Danny in prison. After the trial had finished, he thanked me for coming and told me he never wanted to see me again all in the same breath. I hold on to the hope that one day he might change his mind, but for now, I stay away. I would love to be able to tell him that I know the truth; or at least, I know half of the truth. I don't know how Danny's prints found their way onto that knife, nor how his t-shirt was found covered in her blood. I don't know if he wanted to kill Ayla or whether he would have done it himself on another night. But I do know that Danny is not a murderer. And I do know that it was Lily who killed Ayla that night.

Danny

Life inside is up and down. I guess just like life on the outside too in that sense. There were days when I felt at home here, when the guards were in a good mood and my mates and I could hang out for lunch and chat shit and play games. And there were days when I felt homesick, when words got twisted and someone had to prove themselves. And those days weren't so easy. Everyone in here is innocent. Or in the very least, their victim 'deserved it', whatever the hell that means. I've been in here for just over five years now so I've seen my fair share of people coming and going, and then unsurprisingly, coming back in again. No one changes in here. They just get further and further entrenched in their view of the world they already held. I guess that's like life on the outside too.

Every night before I fall asleep, I pray that my subconscious will give me a rest from the torture. During the day, I can bat away the thoughts more easily than in my sleep. But it's when I'm deeply dreaming that the memories squeeze my mind, twisting my brain so fiercely that I wish it would break.

Sometimes, like tonight, the torture clamps down before I have even fallen asleep. It's as if it lingers, patiently biding its time until all my guards are down. And then it springs, suffocating me with all of the moments I wish I could forget.

That day had started off pretty shitty. I had woken up and realised that Mum was going to be out of it again, just like she had sworn blind she wouldn't be. I don't know why I still believed her after all of this time. I woke up that day feeling so angry at the world for how my life was something I didn't feel like it should be. I didn't deserve this. It was always on my birthdays when I had this strange yearning to see dad. And that yearning always made me feel so feeble. I shouldn't miss him. I didn't have the right to, not after all of the nights I had prayed that he would disappear. I couldn't make sense of how I could so deeply despise him and yet still feel such an ache in my heart for where he should be. I was eighteen now and I had hoped that the yearning would no longer be there. I had prayed that this was the year that I would feel differently. But still, I woke up with that inevitable longing deep in my chest, which burned so intensely in all of the wrong ways.

I was feeling confused and pissed off and sorry for myself. And then I heard a knock on my door and Lils came into my room and everything just seemed brighter all of a sudden. She sat on the end of my bed and we chatted about nothing and her being there in those moments was the best birthday present I could have ever asked for. Her, being there in those moments, promised me that I mattered. I was so grateful. I don't think Lily ever realised how I needed her just as much as she needed me. We grabbed our coats and headed to the Red Dragon down the road. We parked up in the corner and had a proper laugh with my mates. It didn't feel like having my little sister there but instead just another friend. It was turning out to be an alright birthday after all. It was a couple of hours into the session when Ayla walked over to our table. I immediately felt my heart sink, knowing that wherever Ayla went, drama tended to follow. But as she walked over with Lil's by her side, I saw the unmissable twinkle in Lily's eyes. I knew what was going on between them. I had known for a few months now and I hadn't wanted to admit it but there was no hiding that look. I smiled, because despite everything, despite all the prejudice and the stick I would get from my mates, despite my feelings towards Ayla and my feeling that she was bad news, despite all of that, Lily was happy. And that was truly all I cared about.

The rest of the time at the pub had all been a little bit blurry to say the least. My mates had been buying me drinks all night and I had done more shots than I had wanted to. I had performed the obligatory, 'oh no I can't do another one' before immediately guzzling it down. It had been a good birthday. I had felt young and silly and loud and how everyone should have the chance to feel at eighteen years old. I hadn't felt a moment in time passing like it did before then. It was like my brain knew that this was the end of my normal. It was like I knew that I had to savor every lasting moment of a time before now.

When the pub had eventually closed, I desperately tried to keep the night going for a while, frantically trying to convince people to come to the club down the road. But the night was drawing to a close and despite my best efforts, everyone seemed ready to clock out and call it a day. After eventually giving up on my quest, I made my way towards the back of the pub to make the shortcut back home. It was only then when I heard her yelling after me.

"Dan! Oi Dan, wait up!" I turned around to see Ayla half-jogging, half-walking, half-stumbling toward me. *Here comes the drama*, I thought to myself. I instinctively glanced around to see if anyone could save me from a moment alone with her but everyone else had gone their separate ways and it almost felt like it was only us two in the whole world left.

"You look after my little sister yeah?" I jovially said, smiling from a distance. She continued to walk towards me and I held my ground. She smiled, a knowing smile.

"And what would you know about that?" she smirked,

"I wasn't born yesterday you know" I paused, almost debating the next question before I asked it. "Do you love her?" She looked up at me and I saw something change in her eyes. It was like a dark mist overhauled them. My gut twisted inside me. I had only ever seen that dark mist from dad before and I hated the monster it turned him into. Her eyes narrowed and her smile vanished.

"The truth?"

"Of course," I nodded. She took a deep breath, as if contemplating how much fun she could have with me.

"Your little sister is easy Dan. She's quite frankly obsessed with me and I've got her under my thumb. She's an easy fuck and a fun

231

waste of time. That's all there is to it". Her words slurred out of her, a string of bitterness she was evidently enjoying every moment of. She was controlled, poised, despite the fountain of alcohol she had drunk. This was the Ayla I knew. No one loved a power play more than her. I tried to control the thoughts running wild in my head. I felt a wave of rage surge through me like I had never felt before. I knew needed to control myself but the visceral fury was blinding.

"Wh-why would you do that you psychopathic fuck", she grinned. Ayla had always loved this sort of twisted game.

"Are you jealous? Is that what it is? I'll tell you what. I'll scream your name when she's fucking me tonight, how about that?" The control was gone. I saw red. My fist swung through the air and hit her square in the face. As soon as my knuckles made contact with her nose, I knew I had fucked up. I knew that I was merely just a pawn in her chess game and she had played me perfectly. I didn't have time to think. I looked up and saw blood pouring from her nose, her hand clutching her face. I saw the narrowness in her eyes soften ever so slightly. I didn't think. I just turned and ran. The pounding of my feet on the pavement echoed the pounding in my head; a cocktail of hangover, regret and red rage which blistered through my brain.

I ran for about a mile, allowing the thoughts to rush in and out. I let them swirl and fester before being spat out onto the pavement as I vomited up the pain that engulfed me. Eventually, I slowed my run into a walk and tried to control my breathing. I continued to wretch as I replayed her words over and over again, almost as if to check I had heard them correctly. But every time I did, I could feel my fingers begin to curl back into a fist. With all of the self-control in the world, there wasn't a world where I could have stopped myself from hitting her. I couldn't help but feel that she deserved that bloodied nose. I looked down at my phone and I saw I had had a text from Lily.

Couldn't find you but I've headed home. If you get any drunk food, I beg you please pick me some up. Happy birthday bro, love ya

A crushing feeling drowned me from inside out. How dare she play with Lily's feelings like that. How dare she hurt someone I love so much. I needed to protect my little sister. I needed to look after her. I sent a text back, typing and re-typing several times to try and sound as nonchalant and normal as possible,

Fried chicken and chips coming your way. You owe me.

Up ahead, I could see the chicken shop sign and I dived in.

"Two fried chicken and chips please, cheers mate". As the chips were plunged into the basket and deep fat fried, I silently made a plan. I decided I would wake Lils up when I got home and we would sit, perched on the edge of her bed, eating chicken and chips whilst we sobered up. I would tell her that I knew about Ayla and her and I would painfully recall the conversation Ayla and I had just had. I would admit what I had done. She would cry and I would hug her and I would tell her everything would be alright. She deserved better than Ayla. And as her brother, I owed it to her to tell her the truth. I could feel the fear rising up from my stomach as I envisioned her face crumbling and the tears falling from her eyes. I wondered whether she would hate me for what I had done.

My gut lurched. I couldn't imagine anything worse than Lily hating me.

"There you go mate", he said as he handed me over the bags covered in grease. I smiled and left the shop and continued my walk home, rehearsing how I would say it. I played out every different possibility in my head. I hated the fact that I would have to be the one to break my sister's heart. It wasn't meant to be this way. Yet again, the anger swirled inside me as I replayed Ayla's words over and over again in my head. I must have taken at least four detours on the way home, each time adding a little longer to my walk. I could feel the chicken and chips losing their heat with every turn I added but I wasn't ready yet. I must have been walking for at least an hour with the bag grasped tightly in my hand, grease dripping steadily onto the pavement.

I remember fumbling my keys as I fiddled for the lock. I remember feeling the warmth of the house swaddle me as I quietly shut the door. I remember climbing up the stairs, feeling closer to the unknown with every step. Knocking on Lily' bedroom door, I heard no response. I held my breath.

"Hey Lils, I'm coming in" I whispered quietly.

As I pushed open the door, I saw the fear in her eyes before I saw the blood. The whites of her eyes stared directly into mine, "What have I done?"

Lily

I finished university last year. I ended up going to Swansea and studying psychology and ended up really loving it which I hadn't expected if I'm honest. I made some amazing friends there and enjoyed throwing myself into clubs and activities I hadn't tried before. I worked my arse off and ended up coming out with a first. I cried on the day of my graduation; it felt like it was simultaneously both the start of something terrifying and the end of something great. For the last six months, I've been working in marketing at a small start-up. It's actually been going pretty great. There are only five employees which suits me nicely. I earn a good salary and I am hoping to move out of home early next year. I thought I might get a little flat near the prison so that I can visit Dan more easily. From the outside, I guess you could say my life is going pretty well, I guess. I go and visit Danny on most days. Even when I was at Swansea, I travelled down every weekend to see him. It's awful to admit but there were times when I resented it. There were times when I would have to miss a friend's birthday or my favourite gig and I felt this bitterness rising in me where I knew it had no right to be. It was harder to visit him at the beginning because he didn't have as many visitation rights but as time has gone by, the prison has started to feel like a second home for me, I guess. The irony of that isn't lost on me. I guess part of the reason I resented seeing him in the beginning was because of how broken it made me feel. Seeing Dan locked up like he is racks my sense of self so deeply. I had thought it might get easier over time but seeing him reminds me of the mistake I made that night, and the monster I became the day I let him take the wrap. Every night before I fall asleep, I force myself to re-live the day. I guess it's some sort of penance for a sin for which I'll never atone.

After the pub that night of Danny's birthday, I remember searching for Ayla to say goodbye but I couldn't find her anywhere. I left the pub in a huff, ignoring the yells of Danny's mates calling out after me. I walked home with a deep rage swirling in my veins at how she picked me up and tossed me aside at the drop of a hat. I had tortured myself watching her flirt with that man at the bar as she twirled her hair around and fingers and angelically touched his arms. I had watched her eyes glisten as he moved his body closer to hers. I had felt my stomach turn as my worst nightmare played out in slow motion in front of my own eyes. I couldn't bare it. I was furious at myself for just letting it happen, for just watching on from across the bar as if I was nothing but a stranger to her. I wished I had had the guts to confront her in the moment but I had learnt so young that it was safer to stay quiet. And so, I had. I had stayed silent and instead let the sadness and the anger and the unfairness settle into my bones. It was that same feeling of an emptiness which had consumed me for most of my childhood. That same sense of powerlessness which felt so cruel.

I fell into bed that night with fury swaddling my body, wrapping it up so tightly I couldn't breathe. As I lay on my back with my heart beating out of my chest, I could feel the rage slowly dissipating into the night air and I wished that I could hold onto it for just a little while longer. I knew that as soon as I let the night swallow the anger, it would spit back out a hollow, deep and painful sadness. As the fury was washed away, a deep pressure squeezed my brain. I was flooded with memories of sweaty bodies entangled as one; of mid-winter picnics in over-sized coats; of hysterical laughter that one day in June. I couldn't bear the idea that our memories might end. I couldn't bear the idea that the only thing left of us may be nothing more than a heart-breaking nostalgia of a time before now. It felt like the biggest injustice to a love that was so deep.

It was as if time slowed and the universe let me pause time for just a moment or two. I so desperately longed to feel the anger again but instead, I felt like the memories of us were coercing me into a forgiveness I didn't want to give. It was in those moments lost in time that I realised that there was none of *me* left. It was in those frozen moments that it dawned on me that I had always been controlled. Every choice I made had never felt like my own. Everything I was and everything I wanted to be was so deeply sewn into Ayla. I had clutched onto her so firmly, desperately hoping that she could save me from a past I didn't know I was trapped in. I was addicted to her. So much so that I simply couldn't imagine a future without her in it. I didn't want to know a version of myself that didn't involve her. It felt so dangerous to need someone as much as I needed her.

Finally, after I pressed play again on the passage of time, I allowed myself to succumb to the exhaustion. My eyes weighed heavy and my brain felt like as though it might decay into oblivion if I didn't let it rest. It can't have been more than ten minutes later when I was woken by the sound of the call. With weary eyes, I glanced at the screen and saw Ayla's name flash up. Instinctively, I picked up the phone and heard the panic writhing in her voice, her voice rasping and frantic.

"You need to meet me. Our place. Five minutes Lily. It's important. I have to tell you something". That was it. She hung up. She didn't give me a second to ask her what it could be about or why it was so urgent or why she sounded so different. She didn't give me a chance to express my anger towards her. She didn't give me a moment to decide how I wanted to respond. So, I didn't. I just threw on the clothes I had been wearing which were strewn messily on the floor and I pelted down the stairs. As I passed the kitchen on the way to the front door, I paused. It was as if a magnet was drawing me in. A current of electricity pulsated through me. I couldn't tell you why I picked up that kitchen knife. It was staring at me from across the room, daring me to dance in a world I shouldn't. I still don't know why I picked up that knife. It's almost as if that part of the night is blurry, glazed over in some way. I try to piece it back together now. I try to justify it in any way that I can. I guess it might have been that I was scared of the tone I heard in Ayla's voice. I guess I thought that she might be in trouble. I tell myself now that I took that knife to protect her somehow. I shoved it into my pocket and slammed the front door shut. There's not a day that goes by when I don't regret that spurof-the-moment decision. There's not a day that goes by that I wish I could un-pixelate that memory somehow.

I ran all the way to our spot. The midnight air was icy cold and the howling wind drowned out any thoughts I might have had. I didn't see one other person as I ran along the cobbled streets and through the park that night. It was as if the rest of the world was sleeping, hiding from the nightmare that was about to unfold. As I approached her in the darkness of the trees, I could immediately see her face didn't look the same. She had a bruise swelling by her left eye and there was dried blood beneath her nose. She didn't look fragile or in any way broken. She stood tall, almost as if proud of the scars she carried. I felt a pang inside my stomach and I couldn't place it. Something didn't feel quite right.

"Oh my god Ayla, are you okay? What happened?" She looked up at me and her eyes turned a misty dark. The park suddenly felt eerie in a way it never had before. Our spot didn't feel like the fantasy it once had been.

"Your fucking brother did this to me Lils". The words couldn't compute in my head; it didn't make any sense. Danny wouldn't do this. He would never hit a girl. I knew my brother. I knew how much he looked down on men who hit women. My brain felt like it was being fried in a thousand-degree heat; her words burning the inside of my mind.

"What, why, what, I don't understand, Danny wouldn't do that, what?" I remember frantically asking her, willing her to admit she was making up some twisted sort of joke, willing her to tell me this had all been some sort of terrible mistake. Her eyes lit up. She was loving every moment of this. She was loving the torment she was inflicting. She didn't miss a beat.

"I told him we were just having fun, me and you. All I said was that we weren't anything all that serious and he just lost it Lils". I could feel the uncertainty swim around in my head. It didn't seem to add up and it felt like I was missing vital pieces of information. I just couldn't fathom a world where Danny would do something like that. It felt like everything was crumbling around me. She continued and I wish she hadn't.

"Look Lily, what is this to you? What are we?" My mind whirred as I tried to catch up with everything but she just continued to stampede on through without giving me a second to breath, "Because I'll be honest with you. For me, it's just a bit of fun. I don't want anything serious with you. You know that right yeah?" She paused, "Like, don't get me wrong, I love hanging out. But it's just nothing serious right? Like, it's not like we're in love or anything". I studied her face in silence, tracing the blood on her face. I looked up and gazed into her eyes; the coldness of her slowly seeping out into the bitter night sky. *I love you* replaying over and over and over again in my head, taunting me with every beat.

I let her words sink and settle deep in my bones. She didn't love me. I was merely a play thing to her and that was all I would ever be. Feelings of powerlessness rushed through me. I was that seven-year-old girl again. I couldn't understand why I was so unlovable, how all anyone wanted with me was to control me. I wanted to cry but I desperately bit back the tears.

"Yeah no of course. Me too, we're just having fun". She smiled as if she hadn't just taken my heart and smashed it into a million pieces. Without offering a moment for me to grieve, she then took my hand and led me through the brambles to our spot amongst the trees. She held the back of my head tenderly and slowly started to kiss my neck. I could feel the tingles dissipate throughout my body. I held her face and kissed her lips so fiercely I surprised even myself. Her hand begun to trace the curve of my back and then gently patter up my leg, teasing me with the promise of pleasure. My eyes rolled to the back of my head, my mind started to swirl and I could feel all sense of control fading from my body.

It was exactly then when I froze. It was like years and years of control were relinquished in those few fateful moments. All of the blurry confusion came into focus and I felt like I could finally breathe. I had never had any jurisdiction over my own life and I couldn't face being paralysed by powerlessness any longer. I could feel my mind sharpen and my body stiffen as her tongue ran over my tits. As she lifted her head and kissed my lips again, I felt a blanket of fury swaddle me. She didn't get to control me. I wouldn't let her break me. She didn't get to tell me I wasn't someone to be loved.

It was like those moments were crystal clear. It felt like the most natural thing I have ever done, almost as if I was on autopilot and the years and years of trauma and pain and fear collided in those fateful seconds. I think back now and it's like it all happened in slow motion. I can picture my fingers closing around the handle of the knife. I remember the way I squeezed it

241

to make sure it was real. I can still feel the rush of adrenaline as I pulled it from my pocket. I remember looking up at her and plunging the knife into her stomach as hard as I could. I left no room for a change of heart. I remember the way it sliced through her skin so elegantly, as if it too wanted to be there. The confusion and panic flashed across her face like a car about to crash. I looked deeply into her eyes. I was finally in control. In that moment I didn't feel remorse or regret or fear. I didn't feel angry or sad. I was overwhelmed by an addictive surge of power like I had never felt before, a crackling whisper of strength that I had always deserved to feel. My feet stumbled backwards and I dropped the knife to the floor as she fell to the ground, clutching her stomach. Glancing down at my shirt, I could see it was covered in splatters of her blood. I felt like I owned her in those fleeting, precious moments. *This is our secret honey.* My god in those moments of her unrivalled fear, it felt like she fell so deeply, deeply in love with me. I would give anything to feel that dancing elation I felt in those few seconds again. Watching her life fade from behind her eyes was the most alive I have ever felt.

But those moments didn't last very long at all. As I stood over her and watched her fight for her breath as she writhed on the ground, the bombshell of reality exploded inside. The beautiful eclipse of a moment in time had passed and what remained was a blinding burning sun. I frantically looked around, searching for what I do not know. I could feel my sense of control quickly slipping away from me and I didn't want to let the enormity of what I had done set in just yet. I couldn't afford to feel it yet. I so desperately tried to cling on to that compelling feeling of power which had swaddled me but I couldn't grasp it. I knew that I would have the rest of my life to toy with the what-ifs of that night. I knew I could cradle regret for the rest of time but it felt far too dangerous to let contrition leak in now. Everything was happening far too quickly and I couldn't keep up with the string of thoughts bouncing and colliding inside my head. I live in those moments, every day. For the rest of time, I will live there; forever broken by a memory I can't forget. I wake in the middle of the night screaming at the sky, begging for the stars to take me back in time. *I don't belong here.* My nightmares are relentless. I see her fading into the background and I want to yell; I screech into the abyss but my voice is silenced by a shadow of someone who looks just like me.

I snap back to the present and yet I am somehow still here; locked in a passage of time from which I'll never escape. As I desperately darted my eyes from one side to the next, I caught glimpses of shadows lurking in amongst the trees. I recognised the way he held his body; like a terrified, fucked up little man who blames the person he is on the world he was raised in. *It's all in your head*, I told myself. It couldn't be him. There was just no way. There was no one else here. I shook the feeling of him away, convinced of a paranoia at my most vulnerable.

I didn't look back down at her. I gave her no apology. I knew that if I looked, my perfect thrill would be tainted with the brush of reality. I wanted to hold on to her fear-stricken eyes which burned into my memory for a little while longer. I wanted to clutch onto the feeling of love which I witnessed ooze out of her alongside the terror. I didn't want to look down and see a dead girl staring back. I needed to protect the goodness of the moment for as long as I possibly could. Because there *was* good in that moment. There *was* a perfection in her death.

I turned and ran as fast as I could, back through the midnight trees and along the cobbled streets. I didn't stop running until I was all the way back home. I wouldn't be able to tell you what was going through my mind on that run. When I think back to it now, it's as though I'm watching someone else's life. There is a blank, just a white noise. As I opened up the door, I rushed upstairs into my room. I sat on the bed, gormlessly staring into the distance. A few minutes later and it all started to sink in. The realisation as to what I had done, the knowing that it could not be taken back. Fear gripped me by the throat and squeezed so tightly it felt like I couldn't breathe. It was then that I heard a knock on the door and moments later, Danny appeared.

Danny

I rushed towards her, panic setting in.

"I, I, I killed her Dan. I don't know why, I just lost it. I killed her. Fuck." I desperately tried to clasp at the nuggets of information, begging them to slot together to make some sort of sense but I couldn't.

"What do you mean? What happened?" She stared down at her shaking, bloodied hands.

"Ayla. She asked to meet me. She didn't really love me Dan. She was using me. I lost it and I, I stabbed her. I think she's dead Dan. What have I done?" She looked up at me with her big, brown eyes, a desperation for me to make all the fear go away.

"Fuck. I killed her. I'm gonna go to prison, I, I don't know what to do and I don't know, fuck." I rattled my brain for anything that might help. I wished she would stop speaking. I remember knowing even then, even in those moments of sheer panic, that neither of our lives would ever be the same again after that night. I remember my voice spurting words I didn't even believe,

"Everything is going to be okay Lils. I'm here. I'll look after you. You have to stay calm". I could see the reality settling into her in real time. Her body started to shake and she was beginning to hyper-ventilate. She was nodding but her body folded over and she started to rock back and forth. It was as if her mind was shattering in front of my own eyes and I was frantically trying to catch the shards and hold them together. She couldn't afford to break, not yet.

"Right. Listen to me Lily. Get in the shower and wash yourself completely clean okay. Put your clothes in the wash now. I'm going to sort this. It's going to be okay. But you need to listen to me." She nodded, looking up at me like a terrified child who needed someone to save them. I was so desperate to be that person for her.

"Have a shower and wash your clothes and then you need to get into bed like normal okay. I need to go and do something but I'll be back soon". Her eyes widened and her breathing picked up again,

"What Danny, where are you going? Please don't leave me, I don't know what to do". I could hear her voice breaking, the splintering of regret. I remember getting short with her then. We didn't have much time.

"Lily. Let me sort everything else. Just do as I say. Where did this all happen?"

"Umm, in the park, just beyond the swings through the brambles. Why? Danny, what are you going to do?" I didn't have time to explain and I didn't want to waste time trying to gain her blessing. There are moments in life which are so visceral, so poignant, that they stay with you forever. Lils and I, in those moments, felt already like a mere grainy memory that would defy space and time. It was a memory that would surely find me in any life-time. The fear etched so deeply into her frown, the salt from tears I didn't know I had even cried seeping into my mouth. The feeling like we were the only two people left in the world.

"Get in the shower". I said before standing up and running back down the stairs, my feet thudding so loudly on the ground I was sure the earth was shaking. I kept running all the way to the park, frantically looking around to see if anyone else was there. I couldn't see anyone. A clarity gripped me. I knew what I needed to do and there was no time to waste.

As I pushed through the brambles just after the swing, I saw her lying there. Deadly still. I had hoped there was going to be nothing there and that Lily had just been having a horrific nightmare after all. But there wasn't time to wish it wasn't true. I calmly walked up to her body lying on the floor, my eyes darting one way and then the next, frantically alert. I pressed my body against hers, feeling her blood seep into my t-shirt. I grabbed some dirt from the floor and rubbed it into the smears. Fear settling in with each passing second, my eyes fixated on the knife which lay less than a meter from her lifeless body. I thought about the traces of Lily's fingerprints which were entrenched on the handle. I wondered whether any of Ayla's would be present. Had she struggled or fought with Lily? Or had it all happened too quickly for her to register what was happening? I didn't know how long it took someone to bleed out but from the amount of blood that surrounded her, I can't imagine it would have taken very long. I bent down and picked up the knife with a firm clasp, willing my fingerprints to etch. I carefully placed the knife into my pocket and again, darted my eyes around, searching for any sign of movement. I hadn't thought the next steps through. I looked at her still body on the ground and I felt a wave of shame flood through me. It was never meant to end up this way; not for Ayla and certainly not for Lily. Life isn't meant to be like this.

I jumped back up and stared down at her lifeless body lying amongst the mud.

"Goodbye Ayla". My chest started to rise and fall in an unsteady panic. I slapped my hand hard across my face; I didn't have time for hysteria. The stinging sensation grounded me and I took one sharp short breath. I half-ran, half-walked to the bridge where James and I used to meet to smoke weed and talk shit. I knew he still came here and I needed someone to find it without it looking too suspicious. If this was going to work, I thought, I needed to make it look like I didn't want to be caught, like I had been clumsy and made mistakes. I guess I was also hoping there was a slim chance that it may never be found at all. I guess a part of me had hoped that maybe, just maybe, this all might just fade away into some sort of dystopian nightmare. All I really knew was that none of this could ever come back to Lily. Above all, I had to protect her.

I fumbled around at the fourth brick in and felt it come loose. Taking off the bloodied t-shirt, I wrapped the knife inside and placed it to the back before putting the brick back into the wall. All the while, my eyes frantically racing in all directions, alert for any sign of life. The idea of being caught now was unbearable. It was silly really, because I knew this would only end one way eventually. But I just couldn't fathom it ending tonight. I needed time to square everything out in my own head. I needed time to consider if there was another way. And in the very least, I needed time to say goodbye to Lily.

Once I had put the brick back into its place, I ran back home, my bare skin feeling the chill of the winter evening. It was only a five-minute run back to the house but I still panicked someone might see me along the way. Thankfully, it seemed to be the silent hour between drunken teenagers stumbling back from a night out and early-rise runners pounding the pavement. I wondered whether I would have been able to pass myself off as a keen athlete in training had someone spotted me. The stains of blood that melted into my skin may have been a giveaway, I thought.

When I finally got back home, I snuck into the shower before letting Lily see me. I figured it might break her seeing me covered in blood. I was worried she may fuck everything up before it had even begun. I watched as the hot water peeled the stickiness away from my skin. The water droplets and blood swirled and merged into one another on the floor of the shower. *Blood runs thicker than water.* I watched on as they welded into one another like old friends. I watched on as the water tore away the blood that remained stuck to the ceramic base of the shower. I watched on as the water steadily fell and the final remnants of blood washed so beautifully away down the drain. When I eventually turned the tap off, I stood still, my naked body beginning to shiver. Opening the door, I reached for my towel and swaddled it around my body. It swallowed me like a child and I had a deep yearning to be held.

Once I was dressed, I cautiously crept over to Lily's bedroom, hoping I might find her sound asleep. But as I peered through the crack in the door, I saw her sat on the side of the bed, eyes wide and staring into the abyss; like a deer trapped by headlights. It was so rare to see anyone just sitting with nothing; no phone, no TV, no book. It felt so wrong in some way. It was as if I could actually see the cogs in her brain turning.

"Hey" I whispered, trying to sound as nonchalant as I could muster. She glanced up and me and opened her mouth to speak but nothing came out. Her eyes brimmed with tears and I wondered whether they were tears of grief or regret.

"You have to promise me you will tell the police you came straight home after the pub and didn't leave again, okay?" She nodded, her hair still wet from the shower, her eyes still wide and burning with fear.

"And it's really important you look like a grieving girlfriend, okay? You need to go to the funeral and do whatever you have to do, you got me?" Again, she nodded. She didn't speak, she didn't cry. She looked like a shell of the Lily I knew and I wondered whether she would ever be able to re-patch herself after this. I somehow doubted it. I gave her a nod and closed her door quietly behind me. I crept back along the corridor, past Mum's room and back to mine. It was the only time I've ever been envious of Mum. How sweet it must be to not be in this world. Especially tonight.

Lily

I wanted to tell him that I was a grieving girlfriend, that I was grieving for the relationship I thought we had, grieving for the years of childhood I had missed. I wanted to tell him that I was grieving the girl who I was just a few hours before. I knew how easy it would be to grieve. I wanted to tell him how confused and lost and broken I felt. I wanted to say how feeling the knife plunge into her beautiful skin was simultaneously the most traumatic and euphoric thing I had ever done. I wanted him to tell me I wasn't crazy. I loved Ayla with every part of my being. I wouldn't have hurt her if I didn't love her, he had to understand that. Isn't that what love is after all? It was sure as hell all I had ever seen.

I remember waking up early the next morning and having half a second of blissful reckoning before the gut-wrenching reality shook my eyes open. It wouldn't be long until the police would be round. The sun was rising on our secret and I couldn't stop it. I hauled myself from the bed and pounded down the stairs to the washing machine. Flinging open the door, my stomach dropped as I saw my clothes were gone. I wracked my brain, half wondering if it were possible that this had all just been a horrible nightmare after all. I frantically sprinted back up the stairs and shook Danny awake.

"Dan, Dan, wake up. My clothes have gone". He groaned, opening his eyes as little as possible. I could feel my panic rushing through the air toward him and I felt a sudden wave of guilt that I had dragged him into all of this.

"Don't worry, I got rid of it".

"What do you mean? How? Where?" He closed his eyes again and rolled over.

"The less you know the better Lils. Just consider it dealt with". I wanted to push him to give me more but I knew when the conversation was over with Danny so I bit my tongue and didn't push my luck. I started to leave the room when I heard him stir and he sat up in the bed,

"Lils"

"Yeah?"

"Everything is going to be okay. I got you". I smiled as I turned and walked out his room. I believed him. He was just about the only person in this world I trusted. And in that fleeting moment, I truly believed he could make everything okay again.

But with every day that passes, I live to regret that night more and more. I wake up in hot sweats, reliving those fateful moments I can never take back, that momentary choice that changed the course of so many lives. I have curated the inside of my brain to be my very own torture house from which I will never escape. There are days when I picture opening up my head with a scalpel. I rummage deeply inside and squeeze as tightly as I can. I squeeze and squeeze until the pressure finally causes my brain to burst into fragments so small that my capacity to think and feel and remember is finally gone. I clutch onto my brain and throw it to the ground, jump up and down on it until it is nothing but smush. I would do almost anything to be spared from the thoughts that grip me late at night when the world is silent and sleeping. I am locked in my mind and I wish I could be anywhere else but here.

That night has been warped and moulded and stretched in every which way. The memory of it can be so faded one day and so crystal clear the next. I wish I could claim to have been overcome with by a hypnotic madness in those moments. I wish I could claim not to be the person who so callously killed Ayla Stevens, a girl I claimed to have loved. I wish I could claim that somehow, anyhow, that person not to be me. But the truth is that what I did that night will forever haunt me because I *know* that version of who I am lives deeply inside my soul. Over the years that have passed, I have tried blaming everyone but myself. I have spent nights praying for some other alternative explanation for how I could be that monster. But there doesn't seem to be one that I can find, no matter how thoroughly I search. So, I instead go about my days forever fearful that the monster within me will return one day. I spend every day in an ever-delicate balance; I live every day with the devil dancing by my side; an anchoring reminder of who I become in the perfect storm.

I went to visit Danny again today. I hopped on the bus and found a seat towards the back. I pulled out my phone, plugged in my headphones and started listening to my favourite podcast, 'Dance with me tonight'. The sound of the hosts voice was soothing; monotone enough to feel like music but expressive enough to feel like he had something important to say. I watched as the world past me by. When the bus finally pulled up, I made the short walk over to the prison gates. As my feet trod against the ground, I could feel a knot begin to twist and turn in my stomach. With every step closer to the prison gates, it felt as though it was growing and morphing inside me. I wanted to stop it but I could feel that familiar wave of curiosity flood through me as it always did.

I had never once asked him why he did it, or if he regretted it, or if he loathes me as a result. I guess I had always been too scared to find out the answer. Throughout the weeks of intermittent questioning from the police and the constant questioning from knob heads at school, we had never spoken about it. After that fateful night, Danny shut down any discussion of the case before it had even begun. Usually, he would just change the topic of conversation if he could sense it edging that way. One night when I had been particularly persistent in trying to bring it up, he had stormed out of the house, slamming the door behind him. When he came back hours later, he came into my room and his eyes darted around, as if he were scared someone might hear us.

"We do not talk about the case Lily. Let me do what I need to do. You were fast asleep and you weren't there. You don't know what happened. Don't forget that". His eyes were piercing. I had nodded and that had been the end of it. I hadn't ever tried to bring up the case again after that. I hadn't known what he had been planning. I had no clue he was contemplating taking the wrap. I just thought he had removed any of the evidence. My god, I had no idea that he had actually been planting it for if it ever came down to it. I guess he knew as well as I did that the police wouldn't give up on finding the murderer of an innocent teenage girl that easily; not in the small town where we lived.

I was signed in at the front desk and endured the security checks which happened every time I came. It was like getting a body scan

254

at the airport and my body flinched as the woman's hands rode over my body. I was then escorted through the doors and saw Danny sitting on a table across the room. The visiting room was packed today; filled with friends and lovers, parents and children; filled with all of the people whose lives changed forever when someone they loved was sentenced.

I had never tried to bring up the case again after that night all of those years ago but today, as I sauntered over to Danny at the table in that room, I couldn't not ask any longer. I needed to know. It was eating me alive. As I sat down, I placed his hand in mine and held it gently.

"Dan, I need to ask you something and I need you to answer. For me? Please"? I begged, as if he hadn't done enough for me already. He didn't give me the go-ahead but he didn't ask me to stop either so I ploughed on,

"Do you, I mean, do you like regret- "He interrupted me then before I could finish and I was secretly grateful that I didn't actually have to say the words out loud.

"Do you remember when we were little Lils"? he paused and I nodded at him, willing him to continue.

"Dad used to hurt mum so badly". He took a deep breath, desperately trying to compose himself. "I would sometimes sneak into her room before she could hide the bruises with the makeup and they were so raw Lily, you have no idea. I was so scared for her." I could see tears were started to fill his eyes.

"And then one day, Dad started hurting me as well as Mum. He would grab me round the throat and punch me across the face. He would slam my head against the wall. Sometimes, he would dig his nails so deeply into my back that it felt like he was trying to find out how much blood I had inside. And it hurt. My god, it hurt so fucking much" I could feel his leg trembling beneath the table and I wondered why trauma manifests in the way it does. Tears started to well up in my eyes then but I too bit them back.

"But then, when I snuck into mum's room in the morning, I noticed her bruises didn't look as raw as before and I thought maybe it was all worth it. Maybe mum wouldn't get so hurt if dad was hurting me instead" He paused and a small smile escaped from his face; a tortured, painful smile but a true one all the same. "And then one day", he gulped and I could hear the dryness in his throat. "One day, I saw him staring at you from across the sitting room and I recognised the glare in his eyes. It was like he needed someone new to hurt. It was like an addiction for him. He needed someone new to feel the pain. Again, he paused and looked me directly in the eye. "I couldn't let him hurt you Lils, I just couldn't. So, I grabbed his favourite whisky glass from the cupboard and I smashed it onto the floor. The glass went everywhere. My god he was so fucking mad". His smile widened then, as if he was getting a kick out of the fury that he had seen. But just as quickly as his smile came, it disappeared and he continued,

"That night he took the broken shards, and he sliced me with each and every one." I could feel the tears brimming from my eyes now but I refused to let them break the surface. "Smashing that glass protected you Lily". He paused and looked me straight in the eye, squeezing my hand as he did, "I will never regret the whisky glasses I have broken for you. Never".

Danny

Lily thanked me and gave me a hug which felt like it might just heal every part of me that had ever been broken. I thanked her for coming and she was escorted back out of the visiting room. I was taken back to my cell and lay down on the hard bed, staring up at the ceiling above me. Lily wasn't a bad person. She was my little sister. She was a girl who too, like me, had been forced to grow up in a world which so desperately tried to break her at every turn. We were forced to grow up in a world which demanded we treat deep wounds like minor scabs. The world won its game against Lily.

When I was finally back in my cell, I thought back to the day of the shattered whisky glass. I remembered the visceral sting as the air seeped in through my skin and the blood oozed out of me, painting my bed in a dark shade of maroon. I remember waking up the next morning and tracing my finger over the incisions across my arms, wondering whether they would ever look the same again.

When I went into school that morning, my teacher told me off for shouting in the corridor and kept me in at break time for not doing my homework the night before.

When she saw the cuts on my arm, she asked me where they had come from and I had lied and said I didn't know.

She said they must just be paper cuts.

Printed in Great Britain
by Amazon

60961731R00147